Shyla's Initiative

Books by Barbara Casey

Fiction
Shyla's Initiative
Slightest in the House
The Airs of Tillie
Just Like Family
The House of Kane
The Coach's Wife
The Gospel According to Prissy

Young Adult Fiction
The F.I.G. Mysteries
The Cadence of Gypsies
The Wish Rider
The Clock Flower
The Nightjar's Promise
The Seraphim's Song

Nonfiction
Kathryn Kelly: The Moll behind Machine Gun Kelly
Assata Shakur: A 20th Century Escaped Slave
Velvalee Dickinson: The Doll Woman Spy

For more information
visit: www.SpeakingVolumes.us

Shyla's Initiative

Barbara Casey

SPEAKING VOLUMES, LLC
NAPLES, FLORIDA
2024

Shyla's Initiative

Copyright © 2002 by Barbara Casey

All rights reserved. No part of this book may be reproduced or transmitted in any form or by any means without written permission.

This is a work of fiction. All of the characters, incidents, and dialogue, except for incidental references to public figures, products, or services, are imaginary and are not intended to refer to any living or deceased persons, or to disparage any company's products or services.

ISBN 979-8-89022-161-2

For Al

A Note from the Author

Several summers ago, I had occasion to visit a *botanica*, a store that specializes in providing Santeria supplies. It is a place where people go to find solutions to their problems, or ways to improve their lives. Dog-track fans looking for lucky numbers, couples trying to resolve marital difficulties, a businessman looking for a promotion, a mother looking for a cure for her child's illness—whatever the reason, they believe they can find the answer at the botanica. I went for the sole purpose of purchasing a small statue of St. Joseph, as I had been told by someone of the Santerian faith that this would ensure my success in selling a property that I had put on the market several months earlier.

Upon entering the shop that warm afternoon, my senses were immediately overwhelmed by the scents and confusion of colorful objects around me. Charms, herbs, potions, flowers, musical instruments, candles, perfumes and other materials used by the followers of Santeria crowded the small, close space. On one of the shelves, there were three types of cards used to predict the future.

Farther down the aisle from the cards were six different soaps used by Santeria believers to work magic. The one wrapped in red was the soap of love. The soap of money was green, and the yellow was the remover of evil conditions. Next to the soaps were perfumes, over three hundred different formulations, to be used in conjunction with the soaps. The names on the half-ounce bottles explained their uses: jinx remover, protection from the enemy, battle conqueror, prosperity.

Aerosol sprays and candles filled another shelf, and hanging from one wall were the protective bead necklaces called *ilekes*. Back in one corner, a black-speckled enamel pan contained what appeared to be entrails soaking in red liquid with a healthy growth of mold growing over the top. A dead plant stood vigilantly next to the pan, with one branch slightly immersed in the liquid.

As with the mind of a child, a blank slate on which new things are written, I found myself totally accepting and believing what was being presented, without preconceptions. My adult mind, meanwhile, securely conditioned in culture and experience and knowledge, left me feeling doubtful, somewhat amused—and, strangely enough, a little anxious.

Eventually, I found what I was searching for and paid the proprietor of the shop. "You are trying to sell a house," he stated. His Spanish accent was pronounced. Then he smiled and nodded. "You must bury the statue upside-down and facing away," he explained. I thanked him and left.

On the way home, I went by the property I had been unsuccessfully trying to sell, and buried St. Joseph as the shop owner had instructed. By eight o'clock the next morning, the house was sold.

Was it St. Joseph that made the sale of the house possible? Or was it my child's mind just wanting to believe? I don't know. I do know that my visit to the *botanica* on that summer day was the beginning of a journey, one that would eventually lead me to an understanding, an appreciation, and a respect for Santeria. It was also a journey which would lead me to writing this book.

My development has been all within a few years past. I am like one of those seeds taken out of the Egyptian Pyramids, which, after being three thousand years a seed and nothing but a seed, being planted in English soil, it developed itself, grew to greenness, and then fell to mold. So I. Until I was twenty-five, I had no development at all. From my twenty-fifth year I date my life. Three weeks have scarcely passed, at any time between then and now, that I have not unfolded within myself. But I feel that I am now come to the in-most leaf of the bulb, and that shortly the flower must fall to the mold.

Melville to Hawthorne

Prologue

As it was in the beginning, it had always been; and so it was now. Four people, three men and a woman, made their way single file on the stone path that marked its way through the dense foliage of flowering hibiscus and oleander, large crotons, and sweet-scented lantana. Some of plantings were large, some of them small; some of them grew in wild abandon, others in cultivated rows. The plants had been carefully selected, as had each stone, and brought together at this place in this form and pattern for the sole purpose of pleasing the *orishas*, those emissaries who ruled over every force of nature and every aspect of human life.

At the end of the path the four people came to a clearing surrounded by cypress trees, tall and aged. This is where the altar stood. It was that time of day when things appeared diminished in definition and somewhat muted. Colors were no longer distinct, having faded into indistinguishable earth tones. Birds ceased their song, other creatures simply paused as though listening and waiting for the unfolding events of night; and like the disappearing sun far off in the horizon, everything was suddenly less visible. It was dusk.

Miguel, because he was the oldest of the three men, spread the white cloth on the flat stone in front of the altar. Juan lit four white candles, one candle for each of them. Jesus reverently arranged the special fruits and vegetables for the ceremony, pausing in silence between placements. Each offering had been specifically chosen for a particular god. The old woman, dressed in black with an assortment of colored beads around her neck, remained in the background, swaying slightly, her head upturned, uttering words in prayer. Maria Santiago Fanjul was the high priestess of *Regla de Ocha,* that most ancient of African religions from which began Santeria. Known simply as "The Guardian" to those who believed, she and she alone held the sum total of the knowledge, given to her by her mother, just as her mother had received it from her mother before her. That was the way it had always been. It was the only way.

These four had come once again to petition the *orishas*. Unless they received an answer to their petition, there would be no more ceremonies, no more oral traditions to pass down, no more *Regla de Ocha*. Maria was old; soon she would pass. According to the traditions of *Regla de Ocha* it was time for her to give her knowledge and wisdom—the inheritance—to another female related to her by blood. It was through this oral transference, the passing of knowledge from woman to woman, that *Regla de Ocha* was kept alive, as it had always been since the beginning of time.

There were difficulties, however. Maria's daughter had been born with the grayness. The petitions to the *orishas* from Maria to keep her alive had been ignored for reasons only the *orishas* understood and which Maria and her small remaining band of followers did not question. Now there was only one person left who could receive the knowledge: Maria's granddaughter. But she, too, had begun to show signs of the grayness. Soon the grayness would darken, as it had in her mother, until eventually turning to black. Then there would be no one to receive the knowledge, no one to whom Maria, high priestess of *Regla de Ocha*, could pass on the traditions. Like Maria, *Regla de Ocha* would die.

The ceremony would go on for hours with the sprinkling of dust, the casting of shells, the chants, and the prayers spoken in the ancient language of *Gaunche*. Maria and her followers believed. This time, the *orishas* would send an answer. If not, these four people would return again and again, on the stone path leading through the plantings, with their sacraments and prayers, until they were heard.

Chapter One

Shyla Wishon half carried, half pushed her suitcase over the carpet in her bedroom, down the hall, and through the living room, finally bumping it over the threshold of the door leading from the utility room to the garage. She couldn't remember ever being so disorganized before a trip. She still needed to call Evelyn, the lady who cleaned for her every other week, to tell her she would be out of town. She glanced back down the hall toward her bedroom. Hopefully, she had packed everything she would need for her two-week stay at Ibis Institute for Writers.

"Check with the power company and see if there was a blackout last night. If not, call me back." It was Carl, her husband, talking on the phone in the kitchen. Someone from his office was calling about the main computer being down again.

It was barely eight o'clock in the morning, and already the South Florida heat was suffocating. Shyla's hands were wet with moisture not from the heat, however, but from the anxiety brought on by stress. She had planned to leave no later than seven in order to drive the two hundred miles to Naples, arrive there in plenty of time to have lunch with her friend, Jayne, and afterwards attend orientation for the new students who had signed up for her summer course in creative writing. Now she would be lucky to even make orientation.

"Here, honey. Let me get that for you." Carl took the suitcase and easily lifted it into the trunk of her car. "That's what husbands are for." He wrapped his arm around her affectionately.

Another man dressed in greasy coveralls was draped over the front end of her car ratcheting something, from the way it sounded. He had been nice enough to come right over from the garage when she called earlier about her dead battery. She heard him mumble something from beneath the hood that sounded a little like, "Just a couple of minutes more and you'll be good as new." At least that was what she hoped she heard.

Shyla rushed back into the house. She had forgotten to pack her computer disks that contained all of her lecture notes and class assignments from the previous years she had taught creative writing at Ibis. She kept them locked in a small metal box, along with the disks of her manuscripts and other important papers, mainly things that couldn't be replaced if lost in some unforeseen disaster such as a hurricane or flood. South Florida suffered each year from both. There wasn't time to sort through the disks now. She was already late enough. She picked up the box and carried it out to the garage where she wedged it into the trunk next to her suitcase. She would have plenty of time once she got to Ibis to pick out what she needed.

Half an hour later, feeling a little queasy, she exited the busy interstate and turned due west onto a two-lane, black-top highway, bordered by canals. It was called, with good reason as far as Shyla was concerned, Alligator Alley. Gripping the steering wheel of her white Honda Civic, Shyla stared straight ahead while other drivers glared, honked, and demonstrated some incredibly creative obscene gestures of the worse kind as they tried to pass. Occasionally, Shyla glanced quickly at a waving finger, a slapped forearm, and in one instance, a bare ass hanging out of a window on the passenger's side of a car as it whizzed by. Except for the bare ass demonstration, each time she smiled apologetically for her slow pace. But, after all, didn't they realize Alligator Alley was one of the most dangerous roads in Florida? She was just trying to be a safe driver. Unfortunately, Alligator Alley was also the quickest and most direct road that went from West Palm Beach to Naples and that was where she was going.

Shyla's Initiative

A blond woman driving a red convertible sports car that had been trailing the pack for some time suddenly whipped around the Honda in a sling-shot fashion and, having once landed squarely in front of Shyla, slammed on the breaks before once again speeding off. Shyla swerved to avoid what she thought was an inevitable collision, only to immediately pop out into a sweat when she realized the sports car was well out of harm's way. Apparently the woman had deliberately tried to scare the hell out of Shyla. It had worked. Up ahead the young woman raised her hand into the air and waved cheerfully at Shyla before she continued down the highway. Wiping the moisture from her upper lip, Shyla looked in the rear-view mirror and was relieved to see that there were no more cars behind her.

She relaxed her grip on the steering wheel, but only slightly, and took a deep, shaky breath. The pain in her right temple was reminding her of all the problems that had come up that morning. She didn't have another anxiety attack, but she came close. It hadn't mattered to Carl that she wanted to leave early in order to avoid all the traffic and driving in the hot sun. He had insisted on cooking a big breakfast for her anyway, which only succeeded in delaying her that much more not to mention giving her an upset stomach. Of course, he couldn't be blamed for her dead car battery or her last-minute packing. But everything together had put her two hours behind schedule. Now that she finally was on her way, it was a relief in spite of her nervousness about driving on Alligator Alley.

A sharp pain jabbed the right side of Shyla's head and left it throbbing, as though to remind her it was still there. She reached out and turned on the radio, tuning in the classical music station. Maybe that would help. Strands of Mahler's *Fourth Symphony* filled the air around her, for some reason reminding Shyla that she had forgotten to call Evelyn to tell her that she would be away for two weeks. She had also forgotten to leave a check for her. In an attempt to free up more time in order to write, Shyla had hired Evelyn to do light housework for her shortly after Carl moved in. She came every other Wednesday and so far had worked out very well, except for the fact that she loved to talk. Shyla had started locking herself in her office on those days Evelyn came just to avoid the marathon conversations Evelyn obviously enjoyed. "I was studying to be a nurse," Evelyn had told Shyla during one of those conversations, "until an instructor found me crouched in a broom closet crying hysterically. I just couldn't stand the sight of blood. That was when I started cleaning other people's houses. Of course, all that happened before I got married and had babies. I think having babies makes anybody less squeamish. I did the right thing, though. I like cleaning houses." She had done well in the house-cleaning business, from what she told Shyla, and she had all the business she could handle. As a fourth generation Palm Beacher, she knew everyone and everything that was going on in the county. Unfortunately, it wasn't the kind of thing that Shyla especially cared about or wanted to know.

Shyla slowed the car and fumbled around in the built-in storage container located between the two front seats. When she found the phone, she pressed the button for dialing Evelyn's home. Maybe she hadn't left yet.

"Good morning." It was Evelyn.

"Evelyn, this is Shyla. I forgot to mention that I will be away for a couple of weeks, but there's a key under the potted plant on the front porch so you can let yourself in. I'll pay you when I get back, and if anything comes up, you can reach Carl at his office."

"That will be fine," Evelyn answered cheerfully. "Are you going on vacation?"

"No. Not this time." Shyla knew Evelyn wanted more of an answer, but she wasn't willing to give her one. Not with the traffic once more backed up behind her the way it was. "I'll see you in two weeks."

Shyla tossed the phone back into the compartment and pushed on the accelerator—slightly. Several cars whizzed around her, obviously annoyed. Shyla reached down and turned off the radio. Up ahead the traffic had come to a stop. They were working on the road, Shyla guessed. She sat back in the seat and took a deep breath. Another delay.

Before she met Carl, she had been a widow for twelve years and during that time had learned pretty much how to take care of things herself. She didn't always do things right, but if she made a mistake, it was her mistake, and she could usually find someone to fix it. The important thing was that she felt comfortable and settled. She hadn't considered finding someone else to spend time with, let alone live with for the rest of her life. She hadn't even bothered looking. She was content living quietly and on her own. And then Carl Cores came along, lost, dropping things, and a button missing from his shirt. She had gone to the university in Boca Raton to lecture a writers' group, and he had mistakenly come in looking for another classroom where he was supposed to be offering instruction in computers. It was a night class and his first time teaching. Afterwards, he had waited outside until Shyla was finished just so he could walk her to her car.

Over the next several months, they saw one another frequently and each time Shyla was amazed at how considerate, attentive, and thoughtful he was. Carl was originally from Argentina, but he had been educated in the United States. He was just coming out of a marriage of over twenty years. His two daughters were both grown, had good jobs, and were living in their own apartments. His father had died ten years earlier, and his mother lived in New Jersey. All the rest of his family—a various assortment of aunts, uncles, and cousins—still lived for the most part in Argentina. A few were scattered in Spain and Italy.

Shyla had almost forgotten what it was like to have someone she could completely trust and be herself with. She had found that level of intimacy with her first husband. Then when he died, it was simply too difficult and too painful to let someone else get close to her. Getting back into the so-called "dating game" even at her age was too much of an effort. Maybe it worked for other women who were thirty-five, but not Shyla. So she channeled all of her energy into her writing. Gradually Carl managed to change that by introducing her to his culture and some of the things she had never been exposed to. The language, the food, the music—all of it was interesting and exciting, and Carl was fun to be with. He put balance back into her life and added a different dimension. He awakened her passions. Never critical, never pressuring, he allowed Shyla to come to him at her own pace, in her own time.

Naturally she had concerns. His two daughters, Deena and Christine, for one thing. They couldn't even be civil to her and refused to have anything to do with her or their father, out of loyalty to their mother she supposed, and she didn't want to be put in the middle of something where Carl would have to choose between her and his own kids. Finances for another. Even though Carl made a good salary, over half of it went to his former wife in alimony payments. It wouldn't be impossible for the two of them to live on her income, but it would be difficult. Not only that, the ex-wife was still living in the area, and she frequently called on Carl to do things for her. Each time she needed something, it was usually when Shyla and Carl had made plans. Each time their plans either got changed or canceled so he could take care of whatever had come up.

It was because of this as well as her almost obsessive need for privacy that Shyla instinctively pulled back, putting up mental walls and intangible obstacles in order to protect herself from getting hurt whenever she felt Carl getting too close or the situation becoming uncomfortable. But each time Carl would explain the problem away. His daughters were grown now, working, doing well, and had their own lives to lead. They didn't need him and he no longer needed them in his life. Shyla was all he needed. His ex-wife would probably remarry within the year; in fact, she was already dating someone. Then the alimony payments would stop—along with her calls. It was Shyla he loved and wanted to be with. He just wanted to do things for her and take care of her. The pension he would receive once he retired along with his 401 (k) plan would be more than enough to take care of them and give her anything she needed even after he was gone.

He also understood her need for privacy and respected it. That was one of the reasons he loved her so much. He would never allow anyone or anything to interfere with it. He understood how important Shyla's home was to her as well. Not only was it the place where she worked. It was her sanctuary. It was the one place she could escape to when lectures to writers' groups, book signings, and meetings with editors became too much or life in general became too stressful. If there was entertaining that needed to be done, especially since he came from such a large family, it could be done in one of the many nice restaurants nearby. One by one, Carl dispelled Shyla's doubts. In time, Shyla began to believe that she and Carl did have something special, and eighteen months after that first night they met, they got married. Seven weeks and two days later, his mother moved from New Jersey to West Palm Beach so she could be closer to her son.

Shyla glanced at the clock on the dashboard; it was just a little past nine. Carl would already be at his office. She wondered if he had called his mother yet. Probably. She also wondered if they spoke to each other in Spanish the way they did when she was around. Probably not.

* * *

"Then you'll just have to shut it down and try to reboot it. Let me know what happens." Carl slammed the phone down. The main computer was giving them a hassle again. This was the third time in a week that someone had called him at home before he left for work. He was pissed. He missed Shyla already. He just wasn't good at staying by himself. He had plenty of shit to do to keep him busy like vacuum the pool, clean the mildew from the walk and drive, and prune the hedges. There was always shit to do when you owned your own home, and Shyla liked to have everything perfect. But he couldn't get motivated to do anything. Besides, it was Shyla's house, not his, although he did try to do his share of the work. After all, he had moved in with her when they got married.

He had tried to talk Shyla out of going to Naples. She had been teaching that same damn creative writing course at some fancy writers' retreat for eleven some years, and even though she had given up all of her other obligations that took her out of town when she married him, she either couldn't or wouldn't give up this one. "I am under contract and, besides, two weeks during the summer isn't that long to be away," she had argued. "If you can't come with me, then you can take care of things while I am gone." She had laughed at him then and kissed him on the cheek, making him feel like a kid.

Of course she was right. Getting away from his own job was impossible right now. But he still didn't like it. In the eight months they had been together as husband and wife, he had gotten used to her taking care of things and just being there for him. It felt good to be able to come home to a clean house, clean clothes, and a nice hot meal every night. He especially needed her in the mornings when they first woke up. She was wonderful to wake up to, so soft and willing. And wet. She was always wet and ready for him. She was good about running his errands as well, like dropping off his dry cleaning and picking up his prescription medicines. He had enough on his mind with his job without having to worry about all the petty, every-day things. The company he had worked with for over fifteen years had recently been bought out. He along with everyone else employed there was feeling the tension that comes with working for a new owner and the uncertainty of what is expected of them. A few employees, although not from his department, had already received termination notices. Others had either left on their own to find work somewhere else or they were in the process of looking. Company morale was at an all-time low.

The week before, the Director of Personnel had sent around a notice to everyone to update the beneficiary forms of their pension and 401 (k) plans. Of course, everyone immediately interpreted that to mean there were going to be some more people out of a job. He really should have named Shyla beneficiary in both plans, but at the last minute he had named his two daughters instead, reasoning that he might be able to somehow use that as leverage to get them to accept his marriage with Shyla and win them back. So far, nothing else had worked. He could always add Shyla's name later, if it should come to that.

Now that his mother had moved down from New Jersey, that didn't make things any easier on him either. She was constantly calling him at work, wanting this and needing that, expecting him to eat lunch with her every day or haul her around wherever it was that she needed to go. How she had managed all those years on her own, he couldn't imagine. She had worked, driven her own car, and lived alone. Now she had trouble getting out of bed in the mornings. He kept thinking she would eventually back off once she got settled in and learned her way around, but she hadn't. If anything, she had gotten even more demanding. He needed Shyla at home to run interference, not that she could. His mother didn't want to call Shyla when she needed something. She said she couldn't understand her. That was why she insisted on always calling Carl. But that could change. That was what was so great about Shyla being a writer. She worked at home. She had plenty of time on her hands to do whatever needed to be done. Especially since she had that woman cleaning for her. Still, Shyla had insisted on going to Naples anyway. She would be gone two weeks, and she expected him to stay home and take care of things. He couldn't understand why she wanted to go; she could have gotten out of the contract.

Carl wandered into Shyla's office. Papers were stacked neatly on her desk—manuscripts sent to her from other writers wanting her to critique them. A yellow ceramic frog, a gift from a fan no doubt, held an assortment of pens and pencils next to a clean notepad. Several journals were piled in a basket next to a chair—things she would read whenever she got around to it. Nothing was out of place. The fresh flowers he had brought to her earlier in the week were in a vase next to her computer "where I can see them. Maybe they will give me inspiration," she had said. Shyla had been complaining lately that she hadn't been able to write anything since they had gotten married because there had been so many interruptions and distractions and changes in her life. Even though she didn't say it, he was sure she was referring to his mother moving less than eight miles away with all of her needs, and, of course, there had been a few of his relatives to come visit with them from South America. Actually, they had come to visit his mother, but she expected him and his new bride to entertain them as well. It was easier to do that than to listen to his mother complain. To him it wasn't that big of a deal to fix dinner for them or take them around site-seeing. He had plenty of vacation days saved up, and he rather enjoyed it. Showing off his beautiful American wife—a published author, at that—and their big home with the swimming pool. But Shyla considered it an interruption. For one thing, his family ate dinner much later than Shyla was used to. Waiting until ten o'clock at night to eat made her feel sick. Then she would be tired the next day and unable to focus on her writing. She enjoyed an occasional excursion to Epcot or Disney World or any of the other tourist attractions, but when it happened several times in one month, the long drive mixed with the inevitable confusion of having foreign visitors along left her exhausted.

Language presented a problem as well. The fact that she was the only one who couldn't speak Spanish and none of his family, outside of him and his mother, spoke English didn't help. Carl understood how she might feel left out, but after all they were his family. He couldn't very well ignore them when they came to visit. Besides, what did she consider two weeks in Naples? That was an interruption. It was certainly an interruption to what he needed.

The phone rang. It was his office. They had managed to get the computer running again. Carl went into the kitchen where he dumped some ground coffee into a filter, the same filter he had used earlier that morning. It was too much trouble to dig a clean one out of the container from the bottom cabinet by the sink. That was where Shyla liked to keep them. She had a special place for everything. Then he poured water into the coffee-maker and turned it on. He didn't have to be at work for another hour, but that wasn't enough time for him to start on anything around the house. He might as well drink another cup of coffee. He had fixed breakfast for Shyla and made the bed before she left, wanting to show her how much he loved her. She was already running late and he knew she liked things to be in order and in place, like those coffee filters. She said she couldn't function if things were out of place.

Just as he sat down with his coffee the telephone rang again. He knew who it was before he even answered it and considered just letting it ring. But she would only track him down later at the office. "Yes, she has already left," he said to his mother. "Yes, I was talking to someone from the office," he said in answer to her question as to why his phone had been busy. "All right, I'll stop by on my way to work." She needed help in hanging a picture.

* * *

Pilar put the phone down, lay back against the bed pillows, and sighed deeply, waiting to see if her arthritis was going to act up. She had gotten up earlier than her normal time to go to the bathroom and then couldn't go back to sleep. She couldn't stop thinking about her son, Carlos, which was not unusual, and his young American wife. A few months prior to moving to Florida from New Jersey, she hadn't seen or spoken to her son for over ten years. It was all because of his first wife, Ana. That one had put herself between Pilar and her son as well as her two grandchildren. She had caused the problem. Out of jealousy, Pilar believed, most probably. Ana had resented all the time Carlos and his mother spent together, and she had made Pilar pay the price by turning her own son against her and refusing to let her see her two granddaughters. But when Carlos divorced her and married this woman, Pilar decided to make amends. It had been her dream all those years to get her son back, and it was so easy with Ana out of the picture. After all, Pilar was getting older, she was a widow, and her health wasn't what it should be. High sugar, arthritis, a heart condition. And she was severely overweight. She needed attention. If she were to get sick, there wouldn't be anyone to help her, at least no one she wanted to help her and not in New Jersey. She needed to have Carlos close by, and besides that, the harsh cold winters in New Jersey were getting to be more than she could stand. Warm Florida winters would be nice. His new wife, Shyla, wouldn't be any trouble. Not like the first one. Shyla was quiet and shy, even a little stand-offish. She had no, how you say, initiative. No matter when or how often Pilar asked Carlos to come over to help her do things, Shyla never complained. At least Carlos said she didn't. It was a good thing, too, because Pilar wasn't about to let another woman come between her and her son and grandchildren again, even if she did sense that Shyla didn't especially like it.

So now she was gone to Naples to teach at some sort of writers' retreat. Just like Pilar didn't approve of Shyla calling her son "Carl," neither did she approve of her leaving Carlos like that for two weeks; but in a way she was glad. Now she could have him all to herself. She might even suggest he stay with her in her condominium instead of in that big house that Shyla owned. She could fix his supper in the evenings when he got home from work and breakfast in the mornings before he left. She would enjoy that. Maybe, while he was staying with her, he could hang those verticals in her dining room and bedroom that he hadn't gotten to yet. She also wanted him to check around and get some estimates on storm shutters. The last thing she wanted to worry about was her new condo getting destroyed in a hurricane. She had heard the stories of past storms and seen the terrible pictures on television. Carlos could install them. That way, if she had shutters when a storm came, she could close up her house and go stay with Carlos and Shyla. Carlos had told her that Shyla liked her privacy, but if she went to stay with them, she wouldn't be any trouble. After all, she was family, and they had that extra guest room. She might even do some cooking while she was there, depending on how stiff and swollen her joints felt.

Pilar sighed once more, shrugged her shoulder, and glanced over at the picture propped against the wall next to a chair. It showed a matador dressed in yellow silk and velvet, adorned with beads, jewels, and braid. He was carrying a sword and waving his *muleta*, a small red cloth draped over a stick, in front of a bull. It was just a print, but she liked the artist, Francisco de Goya. He was born in that region of Spain where her own family had originated. She had uncovered the painting only the day before when she dug it out of one of the several boxes still stacked in the garage. Little by little she was getting things unpacked and put away. She was just taking her time, not wanting to tire herself out too much in the Florida heat, doing what she could and setting aside everything else for Carlos to do. Right now, it was that picture, and she wanted him to hang it on the wall over her sofa in the living room. If she looked around, she was sure she could find something else to get him to do for her while he was there, before he went to work. He spent way too much time at the office anyway. Slowly she eased herself out of the bed and lumbered into the bathroom to prepare herself for her son.

* * *

Mariela Fanjul laughed again as she thought about the expression of total terror on that poor woman's face when she passed her and hit her breaks. She must have been scared to death. But she had been stuck behind her for over eleven miles, and Mariela was in a hurry. She had just spent the past three days in Palm Beach shopping. Worth Avenue was the only place in the world that had the selection of stores that Mariela liked. Back home at Trégo on Captiva Island where she lived with her father there were only a few touristy clothing shops that carried things like the basic muumuu, tee shirts, and shorts. As a young child, that had been enough. That and her imaginary friend, Eleggua. Now at the age of twenty-five, Mariela needed more—a lot more. And whatever Mariela wanted, Mariela got.

Shyla's Initiative

The Cuban cafe she liked so much was up ahead a couple of miles on the right. She glanced at her gold and diamond-faced Rolex watch. If she hurried, she would have time to stop for a cup of strong Cuban coffee. As long as she got home by eleven o'clock, that would give her an hour to unload her packages, change clothes, and drive to the Ibis Institute for Writers just on the outskirts of Naples in time to meet Terry Sawyer, her family's attorney, and Jayne Sinclair, the president of Ibis, for lunch. She had promised her father she would be there as a representative of the Fanjul family when Terry presented Ms. Sinclair their check for one hundred thousand dollars, something her father had decided to do since his only child had shown an interest in getting her little stories published. No problem.

Mariela pushed down on the accelerator, turned up the volume of a Marc Anthony tape she had been listening to, and switched her thoughts to the short story she had been working on about a Cuban refugee. A familiar story, but with a twist. The refugee was a woman who happened to be the *Iyalocha,* or high priestess, of an ancient religion called *Regla de Ocha,* the forerunner of Santeria. To those who believed, she was known secretly as "The Guardian." Mariela had already given it a title: *The Immigrant.* Most of it was written. Now she would complete it and turn it in for her first assignment in that creative writing course she had signed up for at the Institute. She thought she had done a fairly good job on it so far, but she needed some professional feed-back. After all, she had never tried anything like this before. Once she got this story polished and sent off to some publishers, she wanted to start on a novel.

She rather liked the idea of being a famous author. It wasn't the money that attracted her. Her family had money, thanks to her grandfather. As a young man he had escaped Cuba and Castro's communist control to start his own small farm in South Florida. Over the years that "small farm" had grown into 240,000 acres of cane and a multi-million dollar sugar business, not counting the one-hundred-some acres surrounding the family estate, Trégo. Besides, everyone knew writers didn't make that much money writing books except for a few exceptions like Stephen King and John Clancey, or maybe a Grisham. But she did like the prestige and fame it could bring her. Mariela liked to express herself and be noticed; she liked to feel as though she were on display. What better way to be on display than by holding a copy of her own hard-bound best seller destined to be a blockbuster in film.

The brightly colored mustard yellow and turquoise stuccoed building was just ahead. Mariela pumped the breaks on her small car and swung off the highway onto a gravel and dirt parking lot, stopping abruptly. Dust and loose bits of stone scattered in the air. In one of the two windows facing out onto the dirt parking lot was a hand-printed sign: *Cuban Coffee, Espresso*. Still smiling, Mariela slid from the leather-covered seat, flipped her shoulder-length blond hair, and went inside.

Chapter Two

Several miles back, Shyla struggled to regain control of herself. Her hands trembled and she felt slightly nauseous. It had taken her a while to get through the construction area. "You are behaving like an old woman," she muttered to herself. She wiped the damp steering wheel with a tissue, not taking her eyes off the road ahead, and turned the air conditioner vent directly toward her face. She had been having episodes like this along with the headaches ever since her marriage to Carl; actually, they started about the same time his mother moved down from New Jersey. It was frustrating because she couldn't for the life of her understand why. She had always been strong and quite able to cope with whatever came her way. But lately, it seemed that everything frightened her.

Naturally there were some adjustments that needed to be made in her life now that she was once again a married woman. There was another person to consider who had different interests. She had never been a particularly outgoing person, but that was because she had a more quiet and gentle nature. She was reserved and always had been, even as a child. Carl, however, enjoyed a lot of activity, especially the social kind, something that hadn't been evident when they were dating. There had been a stream of relatives to visit from South American since their wedding, and, naturally, he had wanted to help his mother entertain them. He had also wanted Shyla to help. "We are a twosome now," he told her repeatedly. "We do everything together." But, of course, Pilar's constant presence made it a threesome.

Shyla was trying hard to understand and take part, sacrificing her time and her energy for Carl and his family until there was very little left to give to her own needs. Now after only eight months of marriage the whole thing was getting to be overwhelming and suffocating. She was learning that having a close-knit family was extremely important in the Latin culture, especially a closeness to the mother, apparently. Shyla loved her own mother and father, but phone calls were made between them maybe a couple of times a month and visits were kept to special occasions. And they didn't live practically next door. She had been brought up to be independent and self-sufficient. Leaning on others was not something she would or could do, and she was finding she didn't have much respect for those who did, either. She felt Carl's mother was being inconsiderate and selfish to expect so much, but by feeling this way, Shyla also felt guilty. Coming from different cultures in the beginning had created excitement in their relationship. Now it just seemed to create problems and negative feelings.

Shyla noticed that there had also been a change in Carl's attitude and temperament as well as her own. Before they were married, they had been able to talk about everything, the good as well as the bad. Nothing was unfixable because the two of them were pulling together toward the same goal. Now she had the feeling Carl was keeping things from her, turning to his mother instead. It was making her defensive and suspicious. The intimacy they had shared in the beginning of their relationship wasn't as strong now, if it was there at all. Carl still said and did the same things. He frequently told her how much he loved her, and he usually did little things around the house like help vacuum or do the dishes. He was wonderful at fixing things when they got broken as well. But he seemed impatient; he became irritated easily. She felt a distance—an awkwardness—between them now that hadn't been there before, and it made her uncomfortable and jittery. It were as though she was being snatched from her own life and forced to live another. Somehow each of the many defining layers that she had carefully nurtured and added over the years to complete her identity at this point in her life were gradually being stripped away and sacrificed, one by one, just like the petals from a flower. The person who was left had headaches and anxiety. The person who was left, she didn't even recognize.

She remembered reading once that when someone is faced with a sudden loss of a loved one, the overwhelming feeling is that of helplessness and isolation. She had felt that way when her first husband died of a heart attack. One moment he was healthy and vibrant; the next, he was dead. For months after his death Shyla existed in a state of semi-conscious numbness—seeing and hearing and even responding to everything going on around her, but feeling nothing. That was what was happening now, only she was the one who had died. She didn't want to feel this way or to be left out; she had too much to give. After all, the reason for getting married in the first place was because she and Carl loved each other and wanted to share as much together as possible. But this feeling of secrecy and separation and the constant demands from the outside on her time and energy was beginning to take its toll on her health and her marriage.

She knew that her resentment toward her mother-in-law was building because of Pilar's unrelenting requests of Carl. The woman didn't seem to understand or care that she and Carl might want time for themselves. Shyla tried hard to suppress those feelings, though. After all, Pilar was Carl's mother. They had only just reunited a few months earlier after being estranged for years. Shyla could see how Pilar would want to spend as much time as possible with her son. What bothered Shyla, though, was that she seemed to want to relive the past, without Shyla, and to pick up where she and her son had left off as though nothing had changed. But things were changed. For one thing, Carl was now married to Shyla.

As a writer, it was natural for Shyla to keep things inside of her, avoiding conflict except when she expressed it on paper. She would keep this inside of her and deal with it the best she could. What she couldn't suppress, however, were the headaches which were frequently followed by severe anxiety. Out of everything, the one thing that frightened her the most was the feeling she was losing control. Always before she had a plan on how to move forward, no matter how bad things were—even when her first husband died. Now she felt frustrated and weak. She couldn't make decisions and her energy had plummeted. Looking back she realized she had been struggling with this for over six months, and still she was losing control.

The worst part of it was feeling that somehow in losing control over her life, she had also lost her ability to write. She was convinced of it. Just as she would start to work on an idea for a new short story or perhaps the outline of a novel, something would come up—another visiting relative, more errands to run, another meal to cook, and more bills to pay. There were always more bills. It felt as though a door had been slammed inside of her, and behind that door just beyond her reach was her creativity. She would go through the same routine each morning, getting Carl off to work, the breakfast dishes done, beds made, house straightened, and then go upstairs to her office. When before she would crank out at least fifteen hundred words a day with regularity, now she would sit in front of her computer and stare at the blank screen until the worry of having to run errands or cook dinner took over. She hated it. And she couldn't blame anyone but herself. That was one of the reasons why she had insisted on going to Naples and teaching the class at Ibis. It was the annual summer retreat, and maybe by being around other writers again she could somehow unlock that door. It would be good to see her friend, Jayne Sinclaire, again as well. It had been much too long.

She saw up ahead a restaurant painted a bright, gaudy yellow and turquoise sitting off the road. It didn't look that clean and she really didn't have the time to stop, but she desperately wanted a cup of tea.

Even though it had been only a short while since she had taken any aspirin, she would take more to try to ease that pain in her head. Slowly she pulled off the highway and onto the gravel and dirt parking lot. There was a sign in the window advertising Cuban coffee and *espresso*. Shyla didn't like coffee, but maybe they could fix her a cup of chamomile tea.

Inside, Shyla brushed some crumbs off the wooden bench by the table next to one of two front windows before sitting down. She checked the window sill for any dead gnats or flies, but there were none, which reassured her only slightly. A middle-aged waitress with red curly hair and an attitude that comes with having lived through many difficult and disappointing experiences came over to take her order. Chamomile was out, but she could give her a cup of regular tea. "That will be fine," said Shyla. She adjusted the cameo brooch she was wearing and straightened her dress to make sure it wasn't getting wrinkled since she was planning to wear it to lunch that day.

As she rummaged around in her purse to find the aspirin, she glanced around the small dining room. Several workers, from the road construction she passed a few miles back probably, were sitting at the counter. At another table in the center of the room Shyla noticed an attractive young blond woman staring at her. The woman got up, carrying a cup of coffee with her, and came to Shyla's table. She was tall and thin, wearing a pair of fashionable white clam diggers, a fuchsia pink fuzzy sweater that only came to her midriff, fuchsia pink anklets, and white tennis shoes. Somewhat daring, but sheik. She looked like a model. A wide gold necklace and gold loop earrings completed her outfit. It was the blond hair that Shyla recognized.

"I hope I didn't frighten you too much when I passed you on the road." The young woman smiled, showing her white even teeth, probably the rewarding results of having worn braces at a younger age.

"Oh, that's all right." Shyla glanced down at the table feeling slightly embarrassed. "I'm afraid I made quite a few drivers upset with me this morning." Then, in an effort to explain, "It's just that Alligator Alley is so dangerous."

"Well, it really isn't," said the young woman. She sipped the remainder of her coffee. "It is a straight road, and the alligators pretty much stay in the canals. Besides, the highway department put up fencing so they can't crawl out onto the road and try to bite you. I bet you could speed up to at least 35 or 40 miles an hour," she teased, "if you wanted to." She glanced at Shyla's trembling hands and immediately stopped smiling. "Are you all right? I really am sorry if I frightened you."

"Honestly, I am fine." Just then the waitress brought Shyla's cup of tea and set it down on the table in front of her along with the check. "Sugar's on the table," she said in a way that seemed to indicate yet one more disappointment. The blond said something to her in Spanish.

"Look, I'm going to be here for a few minutes while I drink my tea, so you won't have to worry about getting stuck behind me again." Shyla smiled now. She was starting to feel a little better. Just getting off the highway for a few minutes seemed to be helping.

The woman laughed and put her cup down on the table. "Well, I'll be going then. Have a good trip."

"And you have a safe one," answered Shyla. She smiled and shook her head as she watched the little red car back around and skid back out onto the paved highway. It would be nice to be so self-confident and to feel that kind of freedom, she thought.

In a few minutes the waitress came back over and picked up the check off the table. The pretty blond lady had taken care of it, she explained. Shyla was sorry she didn't get to say thank you.

Shyla's Initiative

* * *

Carl was running late for a meeting when he finally got to his office in the InformAmerica, Inc., building. "You'd better get a move on—they're getting ready to start." Carl nodded at the guy hunched over the large copy machine and hurried down the hall. After he hung the picture for his mother, she had given him a stack of mail for him to look through and sort; things she said she either couldn't read or didn't understand. Most of it was credit card offers, pitches for life insurance, and information on contests—junk mail which he threw in the trash. Before he left she had told him she wanted him to take her to Home Depot to price storm shutters. That would have to wait until the weekend. She had also told him that his Aunt Rosa would be coming from Argentina to stay for six weeks. She would be arriving on Saturday. His mother had made it clear that she expected him to spend some time with her. After all, Rosa was her sister; she was family. It also meant another one of those god-awful early morning trips to the Miami International Airport to pick her up. Why couldn't flights arriving from South America be scheduled at a reasonable time of the day? He groaned out loud. There wouldn't be any need to tell Shyla until after she got back home. She would only worry. On top of everything else, he had promised Ana that he would go over and work on a clogged pool drain on Saturday since Shyla wasn't going to be home. He knew it upset Shyla whenever he got calls from Ana to do things.

He walked into the conference room still carrying his computer case just as someone turned down the lights. Another company was giving a presentation on a new software program geared to integrate and upgrade the various systems that were already in operation but were outdated. This was the sixth presentation in the same number of days. InformAmerica would have to decide on something soon if they were ever going to get all of the business and marketing accounts consolidated the way the new owner wanted before the end of the year.

He glanced around the room to see who was there. As far as he could tell only a couple of people were missing from the information services department that he headed up: Mario Fernandez, who was still sick with the flu, and the new vice president of marketing, Andrea Ramos. It was no secret that Andrea had been hand-picked by the new owner to head up marketing. They had worked together in the past at another company. It was being rumored that Andrea and the new owner had something going on. It was also being rumored that the new owner had plans to move the entire company from West Palm Beach to larger facilities in Boca Raton since they had outgrown where they were.

Andrea was young, attractive, and aggressive. Carl had been asked to share his office with her since he had one of the larger offices in the building and there weren't any other vacancies. He wondered if it wasn't also because of the fact that he was newly married, and with that came the perception that he was "safe." She had been there a month, and without a doubt, she was a heck of a lot easier on the eyes to look at than the file cabinets and stacks of boxes that had been where her desk was now situated. If the move did take place, it would be in September, two months away. But until that time, Andrea and Carl would share the same office.

Carl felt his heart quicken slightly. At first he had resented her being there. The office wasn't that big anyway, and it was uncomfortable, to say the least, knowing she could watch his every move and listen to every phone conversation. She was completely uninhibited and spoke in that brash manner that comes with being overly cocky. She dressed the same way. Short, tight skirts, high-heeled shoes, heady perfume. In the past couple of weeks, though, he had gotten to know her better. They had quite a bit in common. Her mother was from Argentina, but she had been raised in Cuba where her father still lived. He also learned that she had received most of her education in the United States, just as he had. Because of their Latin backgrounds, they both seemed to enjoy the same foods and had even gone to lunch together a couple of times at a Spanish restaurant not too far from where they worked. Carlos had paid for it each time, and that caused the joint checking account that he and Shyla shared for household expenses to be overdrawn at the end of the month. Shyla didn't question him about it. She just said they would have to watch what they were spending a little more closely. Andrea was married, but she apparently was having some problems. She hadn't told him she was planning to be out of the office. He hoped there wasn't anything wrong.

The pager attached to his belt vibrated. He slipped it out of its case and read the message. *I have arrived safely at Ibis. Call you tonight. I love you. Shyla.*

Carl replaced the pager in its holder. When he got back to his office after the presentation he would try calling his older daughter again. She had barely spoken to him in the entire eight months he and Shyla had been married, but she was starting to come around. He would just be patient. Once she got over being mad at him for getting remarried, he would start working on getting her to accept Shyla. His younger daughter would be easier to deal with once he won over her sister. He would work on her later.

* * *

Pilar finished drying the coffee cups and put away what remained of the pastries. She really shouldn't be eating sweets because of her weight problem, not to mention her high sugar levels, but these were filled with *dulce de leche* and were especially good. She had bought them from a little Guatemalan bakery not too far from where she lived. The picture looked nice hanging over the sofa, although if she had been hanging it, she would have positioned it a little more to the left. Still, it looked nice. She sat in a chair opposite the wall where the picture was hanging so she could look at it and plan her day. She had on her house dress, the purple one that Carlos had given her on Mother's Day, but there wasn't any need to change. She really didn't have anywhere she wanted to go. She had hoped Carlos would take the day off and help her unpack some more of those boxes in the garage, but he had to attend some sort of presentation at work. He said he wouldn't be spending the night with her either, but that he would stop by after work to eat some supper. She had just gone to the grocery store the day before, so she had plenty of things to cook. Maybe she would make some home-made manicotti stuffed with spinach and minced ham. That was one of his favorite foods, and she doubted if Shyla ever fixed anything like that. Carlos had told her that Shyla didn't like to cook much. Since Shyla wasn't going to be there, she would like to call her granddaughters to see if they would like to come too. That would be nice. Just the family sitting down to a good meal together. This is what she had dreamed of all those years when she and Carlos had lost touch with one another. It had been over ten years since she had seen her grandchildren, all because of that hateful woman Carlos had once been married to; and now they were grown and no longer living at home. She had missed out on so much; things like birthdays and holidays, and graduation from high school. Things that as their grandmother she should have been involved in.

As soon as Pilar moved to Florida, she had suggested planning some sort of occasion for all of them to get together, a reunion, but Carlos had told her to wait awhile. The children weren't used to his being married yet, nor had he told them their grandmother was now living in West Palm Beach. He needed a little time to prepare them. Pilar sighed. Carlos better not take too much time. She wasn't getting any younger. And it really galled her whenever her sister called from Argentina to tell her about all the things her grandchildren were doing for her: taking her to this place and that; cooking her food; giving her gifts; visiting her every day. Now that Pilar was not only living in Florida but in the same town as her son and her granddaughters, she wanted to be able to tell her sister what all they were doing for her. She sighed again. If Carlos didn't plan something for her and her grandchildren by the time her sister came to visit on Saturday, she would take the matter into her own hands and Carlos would just have to accept it. After all, how difficult could it be? She had never done anything to her grandchildren to cause them to dislike her. Of course, their mother might have poisoned their minds against her. But she could fix that, once she saw them again. And if for any reason they still didn't want to accept her, she could always mention her will. They stood to inherit quite a chunk of money if they treated her right. Shyla didn't need to know anything about it. She wasn't family anyway. Not really.

Pilar shuffled over to the refrigerator and took out a frozen package of spinach. She would make the stuffed manicotti for supper. She would also tell Carlos to plan a nice dinner out somewhere for the two of them and her two granddaughters. If they didn't like Shyla, then what better time for them to get together with their father and grandmother than while Shyla was away.

* * *

Mariela sped down the narrow tree-lined lane past the bank of bougainvillea, the koi pond, the ixora hedges, and over the concrete bridge buffeted with night-blooming jasmine until she seemed to explode from the thick tropical growth onto a large open circular drive. This was

Trégo. Instead of stopping in front of the wide overhang at the main entrance into the home, she continued past it and around to the left wing where there was another entrance. She skidded to a complete stop inches from the oolite wall that served as a barrier to the courtyard beyond. This was where she lived. Shortly after her mother died, she had returned to Trégo, the place where she had been born, after living abroad for ten years. Her father was thrilled with her decision to return home, but Mariela was still tentatively feeling her way. It wasn't that she didn't love Trégo or her father. It was just that nothing seemed to hold her attention, at least not for very long. A restlessness that had been with her since early childhood would wash over her in waves so persistently at times that eventually she would have to move on to a new place, find new people, new activities, and different surroundings. For now, however, the restlessness was subdued, and she was trying to fill a void that her mother's death had left in her father's life by living at Trégo. She was holding her own, quite possibly because of her new interest in writing.

For the sake of privacy, Mariela had taken over the west wing, preferring to live there rather than in the main house. It was perfect for her. Trégo was positioned on a small peninsula jutting out between the intracoastal waterway and the ocean, and the west wing offered the kind of beauty and solitude and space that Mariela wanted if she were going to develop the discipline she needed to become a good writer. There was a private entrance, of course, and a large living area with high vaulted ceilings, Mexican tile floors, Spanish archways, and a brick fireplace. She had converted one of the guest rooms into an office. Two walls of floor-to-ceiling windows faced the intracoastal on one side and on the other, a stand of cypress which concealed the two-story apartment house where the full-time domestic help at Trégo lived as well as the garden, a couple of outbuildings, and a fenced area for chickens and small animals.

The evening meals Mariela would usually eat with her father up at the main house if she didn't have other plans, but the rest of the time she would prepare her own food, whenever and whatever she felt like having, in the modern, lavender-colored kitchen leading to a screened-enclosed sun porch overlooking the ocean beyond. For the first time in her life, she actually felt excited about getting up in the mornings and "going to work." Of course, going to work meant walking down the hall and into her office where she would let her imagination take over while she keyed it into her computer. But for the first time in her life she felt she had something important to say, and writing it down made her feel like she was finally accomplishing something worthwhile. Strangely, she also felt a sense of urgency about it.

Mariela didn't bother putting the car away since she would be leaving again shortly. She backed her car up to the front entrance draped with purple wisteria and grabbed as many of the packages as she could carry from the trunk of the car.

"RaRa! RaRa!" As she yelled, an elderly woman came rushing from the kitchen wiping her hands on the apron tied around her waist. Except for the apron and a string of blue and white beads around her neck, she wore all black. When she saw Mariela, she smiled, touched her beads, and then hurried outside to gather the rest of the packages from the car. Her name was Maria, and she had been the personal maid to Mariela's mother for as long as they had lived at Trégo. She had taken care of Mariela from the time she was a baby as well, which was when she had acquired the nickname RaRa, and had watched her grow into a beautiful young woman. Like the others living and working at Trégo, she had come from Cuba. When Mariela returned to Trégo shortly after her mother's death, it was only natural that Maria once again take care of her, just as she had taken care of her mother before her.

"I want to wear my dark blue silk suit," Mariela said rushing into the bedroom pulling off clothes and dropping them on the floor.

RaRa put down the remainder of the packages and immediately went into one of the walk-in closets to find the suit. Meanwhile, Mariela pulled from various drawers and shelves a blue bra, blue panties, sheer blue stockings, and blue pumps. She freshened her makeup, brushed her hair away from her face fastening it with combs, and finally dumped the contents of her brown leather purse with the shoulder strap into the dark blue clutch purse. The whole time RaRa clucked over her in Spanish, picking at invisible lint, straightening the hem on her skirt, fastening a button, until Mariela was dressed.

Mariela didn't say anything about the clothes on the floor or the many shopping bags spilling their contents all about. She knew RaRa would take care of everything. Mariela kissed her quickly on the cheek and rushed back out the door. Flipping her hair, she glanced at her wristwatch. She had just enough time to make her luncheon meeting; that is, if she didn't run into much traffic going into Naples.

* * *

Back outside, RaRa's smile vanished as she watched Mariela disappear down the lane. Once more her fingers touched the blue and white beads, the *yemaya* beads, protector of women. The enveloping grayness that had surrounded Mariela since infancy was getting more dense. Soon it would turn black. RaRa reached into her apron pocket and fondled the cowrie shell she always kept with her. Tonight she and the others once again would petition the all-powerful *Olodumare* and the *orisha, Oya,* to remove the darkness from around Mariela. Tonight they would begin the invocation of *Olurun* by beating the drums. Believing as they did in the powers of Santeria, it was the only way. Sighing deeply, she went back into the west wing to straighten up Mariela's clutter.

Chapter Three

The guard at the gate checked off Shyla's name from a printed list fastened to a clipboard, handed her a parking pass to be placed in the windshield, the information packet, and the key to the cottage where she would be staying for the next two weeks. Each of the cottages where the visiting faculty stayed were named after famous authors. Shyla always stayed in the same one: cottage number seven, the Hemingway Cottage. Jayne Sinclaire, who had been named the new president at Ibis twelve years earlier, let Shyla pick out the one she wanted to stay in that first summer she taught at the retreat. Shyla had picked the Hemingway Cottage, mainly because it was slightly removed from the rest of the campus and more private. The cottage itself was little more than a one-room efficiency, but it was comfortably furnished with everything Shyla needed for her short stay. It suited her.

Ibis had been started in the 1930s as an experimental school, similar to the Black Mountain College located in the rural mountain community of North Carolina with the same name. Through the years various avant-garde writers were drawn to the school, creating a link between the Black Mountain poets, the San Francisco Renaissance writers, and the Beat writers of Greenwich Village. Allen Ginsberg, Jonathan Williams, and Robert Creely, to name only a few, each left their influence. Shyla, from the very beginning, had felt a special connection to Ibis; even more so now.

Shyla had made good time on Alligator Alley after all, but because it was getting close to noon, she decided to unpack her things later. She quickly glanced at the schedule enclosed with the information packet. Orientation for the incoming students would be held that afternoon, and there would be an informal rap session for students and instructors later

Shyla's Initiative

that evening. She would have lunch with Jayne and then have plenty of time afterwards to get settled before orientation.

Shyla parked in front of the administration building, slipped on the gray bolero jacket that matched her dress, and went inside. Mrs. Fowler, the receptionist, immediately recognized Shyla and greeted her with a smile. "It is nice to see you again."

"It's good to see you too, Mrs. Fowler. How is that novel coming?" Each summer Mrs. Fowler had asked Shyla to look over the novel she had been working on. It never seemed to change, and at first Shyla had been concerned that perhaps she wasn't making herself understood when she made suggestions on how Mrs. Fowler might improve her manuscript; things like characterization and theme development and story line. But then she realized that the novel was simply a labor of love and that Mrs. Fowler used it in order to feel connected to the rest of the writing community at Ibis. Getting it published wasn't a concern. She simply wanted to be able to call herself a writer, and as long as she was working on her novel, she was a writer.

Mrs. Fowler reached into a desk drawer and pulled out a folder. "I completed three more chapters on it. If you have time, I would like for you to take a look at it." She pushed her glasses up higher on her nose.

"I'll be happy to. I'll get it from you after lunch."

She nodded and slipped the folder back into the drawer. "Ms. Sinclare is expecting you, so go right on in."

Shyla opened the door into the President's office and was surprised to see Jayne talking to two other people. "Oh, excuse me. I didn't realize you were busy."

"Shyla! We have been talking about you. Come in this very minute and let me look at you."

Shyla hugged her friend and laughed. "I am afraid I am a year older since I was last here and showing every bit of it."

"Nonsense." Jayne held Shyla at arm's length and looked at her closely. Always one to say exactly what was on her mind, she added, "Maybe not enough sleep, but you look as young and beautiful as ever." Then taking her hand, she led her over to the sofa where a man and young woman were standing. "Shyla, I want you to meet Mariela Fanjul and Terrence Sawyer. They will be joining us for lunch today and for a very special reason."

"Please call me Terry, and I want you to know, I am one of your biggest fans." Shyla felt her hand being gently pressed by the gentleman. He was tall and a little on the thin side, and when he spoke there was a heavy hint of a Southern accent. "In fact, I brought your most recent novel with me today in hopes of getting you to autograph it for me." Shyla looked down smiling. She never knew quite what to say when someone complimented her work. Pulling her hand away, she focused on the young woman.

"Mariela Fanjul?"

"You are Shyla Wishon?"

Jayne Sinclare and Terry Sawyer glanced at one another. "Do you two already know each other?" asked Jayne.

"Sort of," said Mariela.

"That's a story for another day," said Shyla quickly, thinking this might not be the best time to get into Mariela's driving, or hers either for that matter. "Right now, I want you to tell me what the special occasion is that you mentioned."

Jayne immediately brought Shyla up-to-date on the generous donation from the Fanjul family. "I hope you don't mind, Shyla, but I have asked a photographer to come and get some pictures of Terry and Mariela presenting me with the check, and I would like for you to be in the pictures as well." As if on cue, Mrs. Fowler tapped on the door and opened it to let in a man carrying an assortment of miscellaneous photo equipment and several cameras draped around his neck. "This won't take long," she added with an apologetic smile.

Thirty minutes later the four of them were strolling leisurely on the brick walkway across campus toward the dining room. "Thank you for the tea," Shyla said quietly to Mariela.

"Believe me, it was my pleasure," said Mariela. "Accept it as an apology for my immature behavior on the road." Then she laughed. "I don't know what gets into me sometimes. By the way, I am signed up for your course. Terry isn't your only fan around here."

"I'm glad to hear it." Shyla wanted to ask her more about her interest in writing, but by then they had reached the dining room.

After they were seated several people whom Shyla recognized from her classes in previous years came up to speak. "Shyla first came to Ibis about eleven years ago," explained Jayne to Mariela and Terry. "One of our scheduled instructors had cancelled at the last minute and Shyla, with practically no time to prepare, graciously took his place. Now she is our most popular instructor."

"Not really," Shyla said quickly, and then to change the subject, "Have you always been interested in practicing law, Terry?"

"At one time I thought I would go into parapsychology. I was brought up in a family of psychologists with a bent toward unusual and unexplained human behavior. But after one semester of medical school, I decided to go into law instead. I worked with a large national firm for several years—in fact, that was when I started representing the Fanjul family, and then decided at the age of forty to go into business for myself. I have had my own firm for five years now. Believe me, getting out of the corporate rat race really made a new man out of me. I handle mostly civil cases—divorce, estate management, wills, and in some instances, cases that involve business disputes—sexual harassment, contract disagreements, that kind of thing. I am not very creative, I'm afraid. The only thing I write is an occasional legal brief."

"Not everyone is meant to be a writer. I do believe, however, that everyone has a story within them to be written." Shyla glanced at Mariela. "What kinds of things do you like to write, Mariela, or is that too personal?"

"It's not too personal when you ask. Right now I am working on a short story. I seem to enjoy fiction more than anything else, although I have written a few poems and a couple of articles that pretty much did nothing but foul the air."

Shyla laughed even though she tried not to. Mariela had such a fresh way of expressing herself. Not only that, Shyla knew what it felt like to finally complete something you had been working on only to discover when it was finished that it was trash. It had been happening to her a lot lately.

After they had finished lunch Jayne went back to her office to "tackle the towering stack of paperwork" that seemed to never go away. She and Shyla would have plenty of time later to catch up on each other's news. Mariela needed to get back to Trégo but said she would attend the rap session that evening. Shyla drove to her cabin to unpack, and Terry insisted on following her in his car so he could help her unload her things. "I have an ulterior motive in doing this," he explained as he grabbed her suitcase from the trunk along with the strong box. "I still want you to autograph my copy of your book."

Shyla dug out of her purse her lucky pen that had violet-colored ink and wrote: *To my new friend, Terry, with all my best wishes, Shyla.* After Terry left, Shyla got herself settled in and then checked over her class schedule that was in the information packet. It had been a pleasant afternoon. Her headache had subsided, and she hadn't felt the anxiety since earlier that morning when she had been driving on Alligator Alley. Coming to Ibis had been a good idea.

After she finished unpacking, Shyla got out the box where her discs were stored so she could start sorting through them. She knew which ones she would need; it was just a matter of locating them. When she unlocked the box, she noticed a plain, legal-sized envelope that hadn't been there previously. It had been stuffed between some other papers and envelopes, and in it there was a form signed and dated by Carl the week before confirming to the personnel department of the company he worked for that both his pension and his 401 (k) plan should be equally divided between his two daughters in the event of his death. Shyla's name didn't appear anywhere. She closed the box and relocked it before realizing she had forgotten to take out the discs.

It was a shock, first of all, to know that her husband had prepared the document without mentioning it to her. And it was equally disturbing that he left nothing to Shyla, especially after he had insisted that everything would belong to her in the event of his death. It wasn't the money; she had managed quite well before she ever met Carl. But it was certainly symbolic of what her position was in his scheme of things. Now, once again, the loving faith and trust she had felt for Carl in the beginning was being eroded by doubt, and it hurt. In the short time they had been married, he had contributed very little to their household expenses. She never questioned him about how he spent his money. He just never seemed to have any. Shyla had assumed full responsibility for all their bills, and what little savings she had managed to put away in the past were now almost depleted. Carl had to realize it, and out of decency, if not love, should have given her at least part of whatever retirement benefits he was entitled to.

She decided not to say anything to Carl about it. After all, what could she say? Why don't you want me to have any of your retirement benefits? Like the problem with his mother and the other difficulties she was discovering in their marriage, she would find some way to deal with them. But once again another doubt had been raised and no matter how hard she tried to block it out, the question kept surfacing: *Does he really love me?*

* * *

Once back in his office, Terry found it difficult to concentrate. He kept thinking about lunch and the conversation with Jayne, Mariela, and Shyla. Especially Shyla. He hadn't wanted to gush too much, it obviously made her feel uncomfortable, but the truth was, he really was a huge fan. He seemed to get so much from her writing. Even before she had written any adult novels and she was writing mainly for literary journals and the children's market he had read her work. He had also seen her interviewed several times on public television. He found her writing like her personality to be strong and intense in a sort of quiet understatement. It revealed a sensitivity and deep understanding of human nature unlike any other author he had ever read. Now after having met her, what he thought he knew about her was confirmed. Her writing seemed to mirror her personality. She was soft-spoken, yet interesting. Her opinions were intelligent and to the point, but spoken with kindness. He also noticed that she was shy almost to the point of being an introvert, always directing the conversation away from herself and onto others, but he wasn't sure if this was due to shyness or some deep inner strength and confidence that comes with self-knowledge.

Probably the most revealing characteristic about her was her insatiable curiosity. After thinking about it, he had really blabbed on quite a bit about himself, something he rarely did, but it was because she had seemed so interested. She was easy to talk to. The other thing he noticed about her, and he found this disturbing, was an air of unhappiness and perhaps what could only be described as fear. Jayne had told him she was recently married and, as far as she knew, quite happy in her new life. But over the years, Terry had handled a lot of divorce cases. He knew about the problems and destruction divorce causes in people's lives, often leaving irreparable damage. And in his opinion, Shyla Wishon was a woman who was unhappy with her marriage.

* * *

For her entire life it seemed Jayne had been able to accomplish what she set out to do with ease. She breezed through undergraduate school at the University of Virginia, graduating *summa cum laude,* received her Master's and Doctorate's degrees with honors from Duke University, and an advanced degree in business administration from Wharton School of Business. During her summer breaks and between sessions, she worked as an intern at a couple of the larger publishing houses in New York, first as an assistant editor, and then later in the marketing and sales end of publishing. She was obviously bright, she was attractive, and she had a natural, disarming way with people, which made it easy for others to like and accept her.

From Wharton she went on to accept the position as associate chancellor at a small women's college in upstate New York. Less than a year later, the school's chancellor resigned for health reasons. A search committee for finding a replacement was formed, and Jayne became one of the candidates to be considered. She was offered the job with no opposition.

After five years, she was contacted by someone representing the Board of Directors of Ibis Institute of Writing, offering her the position of president. The offer meant a large salary increase, bonuses, a beautiful home located in the Sedgefield Country Club Estates near the campus, and, most important, complete freedom to run the Institute as she saw fit. The Board of Directors was made up of wealthy men and women, many of them published authors themselves, who were there only to assist her if and when she asked. She accepted the position, and within the week she was named president of Ibis, one of the most prestigious specialized small private colleges in the south.

One of the first things she did was hire an architect in landscape design to devise a plan in which what was then a mishmash of buildings could somehow be connected into a visually attractive and unifying whole. Jayne felt, justifiably so, that Ibis already had an excellent reputation for the writing programs it offered; now it needed the physical, aesthetic beauty to go along with that reputation. The architect was George Dunham, energetic, knowledgeable, easy-going, and single; and eight years younger than Jayne.

Over the next several months, crews of workers under George's strict guidance, moved earth, uprooted trees, and dug deep holes. The end result was a fifteen-acre garden that also happened to be home to the small college campus of Ibis. What before had no form was now defined by walls of stone and painted stucco, connecting brick paths, fountains, palm trees, and trellised arbors covered in blooming bougainvillea. Those months of hard work had brought about such an improvement, not only to Ibis but to the City of Naples as well, that the Chamber of Commerce began listing it as one of their "must sees" in the tourist literature. It was during those same months that Jayne and George fell in love.

Strangely enough, it was George and not Jayne who wanted to get married. With his strong sense of values, strict upbringing, and somewhat old-fashioned perspective on life in general, just living together seemed wrong. But after two divorces, Jayne no longer needed or wanted the bond of marriage. George eventually relented. Twelve years later, and at the age of forty-four, Jayne was still running Ibis, and she and George were still living together.

Jayne sat at her desk signing various papers, making notes to Mrs. Fowler on others, and giggling. It was so good to see Shyla again. They talked frequently on the telephone or sent each other e-mail, but it had been about eight months since they had been able to get together, right before Shyla married Carl. Jayne had been attending a symposium then at the Breakers Hotel in Palm Beach and Shyla had driven over to have dinner with her. Jayne had hoped to meet Carl then as well, but he had been out of town at the time on business.

Shyla, of course, had told Jayne about Carl when she first started seeing him, but Jayne had been a little surprised when Shyla told her she was getting married again. She was so independent and seemed to have everything she needed and wanted out of life. The fact that she was pretty and gave the perception of being vulnerable besides had always attracted a lot of attention from men, both single and otherwise, but Shyla had never returned their interest. That was before Carl, of course, and Jayne didn't know Carl since she hadn't met him. Now, eight months later, she still hadn't met him.

Jayne thought Shyla looked a little tired and perhaps stressed when she had first arrived earlier, but that was probably because of the drive from West Palm Beach. Alligator Alley was a killer, as Jayne well knew because of the frequent business trips she made to West Palm Beach. That narrow road, and always there was some construction going on. At lunch, however, Shyla seemed totally rejuvenated and, as usual, had completely charmed everyone. Shyla was always able to draw out people. Jayne had known Terry for over twelve years, and today was the first time she had ever heard him even so much as even mention his parents and what they did. Mariela was one of those people who didn't mind talking about anything, but even with her Shyla managed to get her to talk about things Jayne was sure she didn't normally talk about. Jayne giggled again. Shyla really should have been politician, but for personal reasons Jayne was glad she was a writer. She was looking forward to just the two of them chatting over some hot tea later that evening. She wanted to hear about this new husband of hers—Latin, wasn't he?

Jayne picked up the phone and dialed. She would tell George not to expect her home until late.

* * *

When the presentation was finally finished, it was almost time for lunch. Carl went back to his office to check his e-mail for messages and to see if anyone needed him. As head of his department, it was his job to see that everything ran smoothly, at least as far as the AS 400 and AMI 800 computers went. Carl had started out in computers when he got his first full-time job in the United States. He knew just about everything there was to know about the inner workings of the machine itself as well as every conceivable program that had been written. This included the new super computer that had recently been installed. What he didn't know, he was able to figure out. His position with InformAmerica, Inc. was an important one, but he wasn't stupid enough to believe that he was indispensable, especially when there was a new owner analyzing everyone's value to the company. It was amazing how many employees had already been replaced by people the new owner had previously worked with. Apparently, if the stories circulating around the company were right, he had a lot more people just waiting for the nod from him to start work.

He smelled her perfume even before he got to his office. Andrea was sitting at her desk vigorously working at her computer.

"You missed another great presentation," said Carl, surprised to find her in the office. "How did you manage that?"

"I am being punished." She keyed in some stuff on the computer.

At first Carl thought she was kidding. "Tell me what you did so I can do it too. Then maybe I won't have to sit through any more of these damn things."

"You cheat on your purchase orders," she said swiveling her chair around to look at him. "Look, you'll probably hear about it anyway, so let me be the first to tell you. I added something to a purchase order after the big guy had already signed off on it. I would have gotten away with it, too, except that bitch Dolores in accounting didn't understand something and questioned it. The next thing I knew, the big man called me into his office and told me if it happened again, my ass was out of here. He didn't even bother to ask me if it had been a mistake. Then he gave me about fifty thousand reports to do for some meeting he is having next week in New York."

Carl sat down not knowing how much of what she was telling him was actually true. "What in the hell did you add to the purchase order?"

"A digital camera—one of those real fancy ones that takes colored pictures under water."

"My god, Andrea, what were you thinking?"

"That I could get away with it." She laughed. "Guess I was wrong. And I thought the bastard liked me."

Carl shoved his laptop computer into the docking station and turned it on. In all the years he had worked for the company he had never even so much as stolen a paper clip. Now here was this woman, not even on the job for six months, trying to rip off the company for a three-thousand-dollar camera. He had to give her credit; she had balls.

"I need to get out of here for a while. You feel like going for lunch somewhere?" Andrea got up from her chair and bent over to get her purse out of the desk drawer. Carl couldn't help but notice the tiny bit of black lace that showed from below the hem on her skirt.

"Sure. I could use some cheering up, too. Shyla left this morning to go to Naples for two weeks."

Andrea raised her eyebrows. "Two weeks? She must really trust you to leave you on your own for two weeks."

"Why wouldn't she?" he answered defensively. Andrea had a way of keeping him just slightly off-balance. He had seen her working the other men in the department, too, but they somehow managed to laugh it off. Maybe that was it. He took what she said too seriously and he came across sounding defensive. "Where would you like to go?"

"Let's go somewhere special. How about that place you took Shyla for her birthday?"

"You mean the Four Seasons?" He raised his eyebrows. "That's pretty high-priced." The Four Seasons was on Palm Beach overlooking the ocean. He had taken Shyla there only twice, mainly because it was so expensive, and both times it had been a special occasion.

Andrea smiled sweetly. "Oh, come on. You deserve treating yourself. Or are you afraid Shyla won't like it?"

Carl recognized the challenge in her tone and her demeanor. He wished he hadn't even agreed to take her to lunch, but he wasn't about to back out now. Besides, Shyla didn't tell him what to do. If he wanted to eat at the Four Seasons, he would. Not only that he had told his mother he had a luncheon meeting to go to when she asked him to have lunch with her. At least this way he would be out of the office if she called. "Let's go," he said following her out the door.

* * *

Shyla's Initiative

The worst thing about living in South Florida, Pilar soon discovered, was the humidity. Even with the air conditioner set on a cool 66 degrees and running all day and all night, she could feel it. Because she was overweight and perspired easily, she had already gone through several boxes of body powder since moving from up north in an effort to keep her skin dry and her clothes free from stains. Of course, the hottest place was in the kitchen when she cooked. Pilar had stripped down to a thin, sleeveless cotton gown in an attempt to stay cool, but even the powder was useless in the kitchen.

Finally the manicotti was finished, and the tomato sauce was simmering on the hot stove. The rest of the afternoon stretched out in front of her. She tried calling Carlos at his office, but she only got his voice mail. He was probably still out to lunch. He had told her he had a luncheon meeting to go to. The more she thought about it, the more she believed that this was the perfect time to get Carlos to reintroduce her grandchildren to her. He just needed a little encouragement, that's all. She pulled out her address book and looked up the telephone number of the beauty salon she had started going to. It was a small place not too far from where she lived. It was owned and operated by a man and his wife who were also from Argentina. She would see if they could take her this afternoon. While she was out, she would pick up a loaf of Italian bread from that Guatemalan bakery that was also nearby and a nice pie—maybe something with fresh fruit. Carlos liked fruit. He had told her he would be there about six o'clock, so she had plenty of time.

After making the appointment to get her hair and nails done, she set the small dining room table using her best china, crystal glasses, and silver eating utensils. Then she went outside and cut three large red hibiscus blossoms to put in a bowl for the centerpiece. Satisfied with everything, she flopped down in her easy chair opposite the sofa so she could stare at the picture Carlos had hung. Every joint in her body ached and she was sweating heavily from the exertion of having gone outside to get the flowers, but she wasn't thinking about that. She was thinking about her granddaughters, Deena and Christine, and all the love and attention they would give her once they got to know her again. This evening she would make everything perfect for her son. He wouldn't be able to refuse her request, not that he would anyway.

Slowly she eased herself out of the chair to go start her bath. She would have to open a new box of scented powder.

* * *

Mariela decided not to drive back to the rap session at Ibis that evening after all. She wanted to finish her short story. Now, having met Shyla Wishon, she felt enormously inspired, even to the point of wanting to eventually expand her short story into a novel. She wanted more than anything to write something that would make Shyla proud of her. She hadn't felt like that since she was a little girl when her mother was trying to teach her how to make *empanadas*. Mariela tried so hard to follow her mother's instructions. At the time she had been too young to read the recipe herself. Working with a large heavy bowl and a long wooden spoon while standing on a chair was difficult. When it finally came time for the secret ingredient, Mariela was so excited she wound up spilling most of the raisins onto the floor. That evening for dinner, however, her family ate *empanadas* made by Mariela. She had made her mother proud.

Now, for some unknown reason, Mariela felt an almost spiritual kinship with this pretty, quiet woman. At lunch that day Shyla had asked about her mother. Before she knew it, she was telling Shyla not just about her mother but about the last ten years she had spent in Europe and her life at Trégo before that. Terry had been just as bad, yacking away in that Southern drawl of his about the research on soul mergers and transference or some such nonsense his parents were involved in. Even Jayne, it seemed, couldn't stop talking about the early years of the founding poets at Ibis. In each instance, it had been Shyla to draw out the conversation from the others.

They were absolutely nothing alike, Mariela and Shyla, in looks or in personalities. Mariela was probably a good four inches taller. There was also an eight-year age difference, Shyla being the older. Yet, of the two women, Mariela felt as though she was more experienced and wise to the world. She was certainly more outgoing. Maybe that was why she had an overpowering desire to protect Shyla. Of what, she didn't know. But more than anything, right now, she wanted to give Shyla something of herself. Something good that she had written. She would finish her short story, *The Immigrant*. She would make Shyla proud.

* * *

Maria walked out onto the patio located off the back of one of the small apartments where she stayed when she wasn't working in the west wing. It was almost dark. Soon the moon would be up, but it wasn't quite time. Saturday the moon would be full. It would be time then.

Miguel, together with Juan and Jesus who also lived in the apartments and worked up at the main house, would select the chicken and take it to the sacred ground beyond the oolite wall and beyond the courtyard to where the altar of stone stood hidden among the cypress trees. All of the other sacraments had been offered. The desired fruits and other smaller gifts favored by the *orishas* would soon be in place. *Ébo*, the sacrifice of a chosen animal, would then be the only thing left for them to do. Each of them had recognized the aura of gray that surrounded the infant, Mariela. They had watched with concern as it darkened over the years. When she recently returned to Trégo after a long separation, they knew then that time was running out. Even in her absence, with each full moon they had without fail made such offerings as *addimú* to the *orishas,* selecting fruits and candies favored by a particular deity. Still the grayness darkened; soon it would be black. There was nothing left to do. It was time for the last sacrament, *ébo.*

Maria glanced toward the west wing. A light was on in Mariela's office. She was working. It was just as well. She didn't need to know about this. She wouldn't understand—not yet. It was something that only the older ones understood and respected. It was their inheritance that they had brought with them from Cuba. It was as natural as breathing. There were only four of them left now; Maria, Miguel, Juan, and Jesus. The other immigrants who had originally come with The Guardian from Cuba were dead. Of their offspring, most had moved on to the American way of life—new jobs, new names, different locations. With no one else to carry forward the Fanjul name, only Mariela remained. Only Mariela could receive the knowledge of *Regla de Ocha* from The Guardian and pass it on to her seed. That way the inheritance would continue, just as it had through the ages. That was why it was necessary for the immigrants to do everything in their power to remove the gray shadow that surrounded her. Once again they would appeal to the *orishas*, only this time they would perform the sacred ceremony of *ébo.*

Mariela had been so excited when she got home that afternoon from the writers school. She had hugged Maria and told her about someone special she had met at the school. An American author. She was happy. This was good. It would give her something positive on which to concentrate, and that would discourage the grayness from creeping into her mind.

Maria once again reached into her pocket and touched the cowrie shell. It felt hot. It had started; the *orishas* were near. She closed her fingers around the shell and pressed. "Saturday," she said into the darkness. Then the drum would start. It would be time for *ébo*.

* * *

Pilar was beyond being miffed, upset, angry, and worried. Now she was panicked to the point of tears. It was seven o'clock, and Carlos was an hour late. She had tried calling him all afternoon at his office but hadn't gotten an answer. One call she had let ring thirty-two times hoping someone would answer even if Carlos wasn't there. But no one did. She had wanted to ask him what kind of bread he preferred to eat with the manicotti: Italian or that round Mountain Loaf sprinkled with white flour that they sold at the Guatemalan bakery. Then she couldn't decide on which dessert to get. She had thought she wanted a fruit pie, but there was that nice flan dripping with caramelized brown sugar that they had just pulled out of the oven. She finally got both the pie and the flan along with the Italian bread.

She had thought of other things she needed to talk to Carlos about as well, and it had bothered her tremendously that she couldn't reach him. Besides that, for the past hour she had been adding olive oil and spooning sauce over the manicotti to keep it from drying out, but the edges were still curling and turning hard. She might have considered calling Shyla if she had known how to get in touch with her to see if she knew where Carlos was. But she didn't have her telephone number, and she hadn't paid that much attention when Carlos told her the name of the place where she had gone.

Her new hairdo was sticky with hair spray and limp from the oven heat where she had kept opening the door to check the manicotti. She had also chipped one of her newly polished nails from dialing the telephone so much. Exhausted from nervousness, she collapsed into the big recliner in her living room. By opening the verticals slightly, she could see any cars turning off the main road onto the street where her condo was located. Already several cars had gone by, people on their way home from work. It was practically dark. She watched as another car turned off the main road onto her street, then into her driveway. It was Carlos.

"Where have you been all afternoon?" she greeted him loudly at the door. "I was so worried when I couldn't reach you. The manicotti is dried out and probably won't be fit to eat."

Carl grimaced when his mother mentioned trying to reach him. He had asked her not to call him at the office so much unless it was an emergency. Everyone was starting to notice how much time he was spending on the phone. But with her, everything was an emergency. "I told you I had a meeting."

"You said it was a luncheon meeting." She brushed some hair from his forehead with her fingers. "What is that smell?" She stepped closer to him and sniffed. "That's not the cologne I gave you."

Carl stepped back holding up his arm so he could smell it. "How should I know. It's probably that new soap they put in the men's restroom at the office." He moved forward toward the kitchen trying to get around his mother. "Something sure smells good in here," he said lightly. "I'm starved."

Pilar shrugged her shoulder and grabbed up her pot holders. If the manicotti was dried out and curled on the edges, it didn't matter. Her son was safe. Now she needed to calm herself so she could discuss the matter of her grandchildren. She handed Carlos the wine opener so he could open the bottle of wine she had selected to go with their meal. If he didn't like the wine, it would be his fault since she couldn't reach him to ask him what kind to get.

* * *

Being back at Ibis and seeing her friend, Jayne, and the other staff members had lifted Shyla's spirits tremendously. She had also enjoyed meeting Terry and Mariela for lunch, and seeing so many of her former students. Whatever the reason, she felt more like her old self. Carl probably had a perfectly reasonable explanation about that thing with his pension and 401 (k). Of course he would want to take care of her. And perhaps the stress she had been feeling involving Carl and his mother wasn't as bad as she thought. She just needed a little break to get back in touch with herself. Having the distance between them now somehow gave her a less emotional and more logical perspective on everything. Thinking back on it, she was sure she had made things difficult for Carl as well. All he wanted to do was please her and, of course, his mother. Maybe the two weeks at Ibis would get rid of her anxiety and then she and Carl could plan their own trip somewhere.

Shyla felt so good that rather than waiting until later in the evening, she decided to call Carl at home before walking over to the student and faculty lounge where the rap session was to take place. She didn't get an answer. Thinking he might be working late, she tried calling his office. When she got no answer there, she decided to wait and try again around bedtime. Maybe he had to do something for his mother. She could feel the anxiety starting to build again.

* * *

Terry shut down his computer and glanced once more at his appointment book. Jayne Sinclaire had asked him earlier at lunch if he could meet with her and the Board of Directors the next afternoon at Ibis. She had called a special meeting to discuss the Fanjul donation. She wanted Terry there to advise them on the best way to proceed in order to get the "biggest bang from the buck" without all of the tax implications and other problems that were usually attached to a large donation. He agreed to meet with them in the conference room the next afternoon at three o'clock.

He had also received a call this evening from someone he knew only as The Guardian. He had spoken to the person just twice before: once when Mariela's grandfather died, and then when her mother died. It was a little disconcerting not knowing whom he was dealing with, but he had been on intimate terms with the Fanjul family for many years and over time he had learned to accept some of their foreign, if not downright uncivilized, ways. The call that had come in this evening had made him slightly concerned, however. The Guardian had asked him to not plan any trips out of town for the next two weeks. His legal services would be needed. An envelope would be delivered to him in the next day or two for him to put with the others, locked away safely in his vault. Of course, he agreed. After all, he was receiving an enormous retainer to make himself available to the Fanjul family as their attorney. And he didn't have any plans to go out of town anyway. He just didn't like all the secrecy. There was something else. He had been brought up on studies of unexplained phenomena and human behavior. As a child he had accompanied his parents on "haunts" as they referred to them. He had devoted a great deal of time in college studying the subject, until he switched to law, and continued to be interested even now. He had a good nose for it. This evening his nose was telling him there was

Shyla's Initiative

something abnormal going on within the Fanjul family, and, like it or not, he was going to be right smack in the middle of it.

* * *

Without exception, Shyla Wishon was the nicest, most considerate person Jayne had ever met. Shyla was a true friend, not just for what all she had done for Ibis or for Jayne personally in the twelve years they had known each other, but for the fact that no matter what, when, or where, Shyla was someone she could completely be herself with and not be judged. They talked on the phone frequently, and whenever Jayne had business in Palm Beach County or nearby, she and Shyla would try to at least meet for lunch. Earlier that spring she had come across a poem entitled *Friendship* written in 1866 by Dinah Mulock Craik:

Oh, the comfort, the inexpressible
Comfort of feeling safe with a person
Having neither to weigh thoughts
Nor measure words, but pouring them
All right out — just as they are —
Chaff and grain together —
Certain that a faithful hand will
Take and sift them,
Keeping what is worth keeping,
And, with a breath of kindness
Blow the rest away.

She had sent a copy of it to Shyla immediately, because it expressed so much how she felt about their friendship. In return, Shyla had sent her a pot of fragrant paper white daffodils.

The two women casually strolled across campus toward Shyla's cottage. The sun was just setting. There had been a big turnout for the faculty-student gathering. "It never seems to change from year to year," said Jayne linking her arm through Shyla's. "The faces change and the names change, but the hopes and dreams of becoming a great author are always the same."

"I know. You know that exercise I usually give to my students that they turn in with their applications? The one on writing a picture book using a cucumber as the protagonist?"

Jayne laughed. "Yes, I remember."

"I finished reading through this group's manuscripts this afternoon, and it is as though I had gone back and pulled out the ones from last year and the year before that and the year before that. The good thing, though, is that always there is at least one exceptional story out of the bunch. Someone has talent and is able to come up with a magnificent cucumber character."

They reached Shyla's cottage and went in. Shyla drew open the curtains on the sliding glass doors so the two women could enjoy the sunset. No matter how many times she had seen the sun disappear into dusk in the past from those very windows, Shyla never tired of it. Then she turned on the kettle to fix them a cup of tea while Jayne settled down on the cushiony sofa, pulling her legs up under her.

"How is George?"

"We are getting ready to celebrate our twelfth year together this month."

Shyla smiled and shook her head. "It seems like only yesterday that I first met him lugging some sort of palm tree across campus. He didn't want the fronds to get bruised so he was carrying it."

Jayne laughed. "I had just been named president, and everything seemed to be going wrong. What I thought was going to be a simple landscape job turned into months of earth reconstruction that was still going on when it was time for the summer retreat. I was terrified that someone would fall into one of the holes George had dug for some plant or other and then take me to court over it. Then one of our instructors got sick and had to pull out. That was when you agreed to come, with your bright smile and positive attitude."

Shyla pulled out a tray and arranged the cups and saucers on it. "I was so happy that you invited me. Besides, even if I couldn't have come, you would have found someone else."

"I don't know about that. I remember one day listening to you and George discussing something about the amount of shade the new hydrangea bushes would need, and I realized that you were seeing the campus not as it was then, all ugly and dug up, but as it was going to be once George finished. It certainly helped my attitude from that moment on."

"Well, some people call that, in the common vernacular, being an air head. The important thing is that George had a vision, and it worked. Ibis is such a beautiful place."

Jayne nodded in agreement. "So much has happened since then. George still designs landscapes, but only enough to stay abreast of any changes and improvements in the field. He seems to be more interested in his gadget tinkering."

Shyla nodded. She knew George had always enjoyed working with his hands and inventing things. In the twelve years he and Jayne had been together, he had managed to sell three of his inventions, each of them having to do with assisting the handicapped in some way.

"Did I tell you I have moved him to his own shop in the back yard?"

Shyla laughed as she carried the tea over to the sofa on a tray. "Is that just a place where he can work, or does he live there?"

"Right now it is a place where he can go to work so that he doesn't mess up the house. However, if he gives me any reason, there is room enough for a bed." Jayne sipped her tea. "How are you enjoying married life? Are you adjusted yet?"

Shyla glanced away, something that Jayne noticed immediately.

"Anything you want to talk about?"

Shyla set her cup down. "It's just so silly and petty," she said.

"You are entitled to think what you want and to have your own feelings," offered Jayne. "That doesn't make it either silly or petty."

Shyla told Jayne about Pilar moving six miles from her home and about the distrust that was building up inside of her. "I can't even blame Carl for anything. He's an attentive husband to me and a devoted son to his mother. He's always wanting to do things for me, like serving breakfast to me in bed every morning."

"You don't even like breakfast, do you?"

Shyla laughed. "No. In the beginning I thought he was just trying to be helpful in a cute, slightly obtuse kind of way. But the cuteness is starting to wear off, and his desire to be helpful somehow only adds to my frustration and anxiety—especially if I have something scheduled and time is a factor. If I didn't know him better, I would think he was deliberately trying to get in my way."

"Shyla, have you ever thought he might be trying to control you?"

"I don't think it's that. He does the same thing for his mother, only more so because she is always asking for something. I get the feeling we are like an act in a three-ring circus. Carl and Shyla don't have an act; it is Carl and Pilar on center stage. Then, maybe, Shyla comes in like a clown to distract the audience while the stage gets cleaned after they perform. I feel so excluded." She picked up her cup and sipped the hot tea. "And then there is his family in Argentina. There are so many of them, and they all want to come for a visit. A lot of them already have. It's left me feeling so nervous all the time."

"Have you been to a doctor lately? It's usually a good idea to start there, just to make sure there isn't anything going on physically that might be contributing to other things."

"Shortly after Pilar moved into her condominium in West Palm Beach I made an appointment with my gynecologist thinking that at the ripe age of thirty-five I was starting menopause. Everything checked out all right. Dr. Viverette, who is a woman roughly my age, has already gone through two divorces. She said I was placing a lot of stress on myself, probably because there were problems in the marriage, and it was because of this that I was having the anxiety attacks and the headaches. She said it was a matter of being confronted with too much too soon, something that often occurs when there is a blending of two cultures."

"Did knowing that help?"

"Not really. I didn't feel any better when I left than before I went to see her. She gave me a sample bottle of herbal capsules, *kava kava*, to help settle my nerves. She isn't a big believer in prescription drugs. She told me to try them for a month and if they didn't help, to go back to see her and she would give me a prescription medication." Shyla ran her finger around the rim of her teacup. "The headaches haven't stopped, and I still occasionally have anxiety attacks, but I'm not going back to her."

Jayne nodded. "Why do you feel you can't trust him?"

"I think because he is always trying to keep things from me, like what he spends his money on or when he sees his mother." Shyla set her cup down on the table in front of her. "And the fact that he has named his two daughters, who don't even have anything to do with him, the sole beneficiaries of his pension fund and 401 (k). I don't even care about knowing those things, but when he goes out of his way to conceal them from me, I can't help but wonder why. Did I tell you that he and his mother only talk to one another in Spanish whenever I am around? It makes me feel like he is hiding other things from me as well."

"Have you told him how you feel?"

Shyla shook her head. "I feel too guilty about it. I should be understanding and grateful that I am married to such a fine man; instead I'm begrudging the time a seventy-five-year-old woman and her son want to spend together. I just can't seem to get rid of the resentment."

"How is your writing going?"

Shyla smirked. "It isn't."

"Listen to me, Shyla, I remember how much you agonized over the decision to get remarried. You discussed your feelings with Carl then, remember? He understood how you lived and felt, and he agreed to it. After all, you are a writer. You need a lot of space. In fact, he convinced you that he felt the same way. So now, he has brought into your marriage a controlling, manipulative mother, half the population of Argentina, and still there is no mention of any relief from the financial pressures caused by the ex-wife. I'm sure his two kids must be hovering close by as well. That's probably why he has named them the beneficiaries in those funds. How can you possibly be in control of your own life when you have so many trying to control you? The way I see it, he is the one who has changed the rules. You didn't bargain for all of that. It is your right to live your life the way you want to, and if he has changed his mind about living his life in the same way, then it is his problem and he needs to either correct it or get out. You are his wife, after all. No one should come before you."

Jayne leaned back against the sofa cushions and the two women stared out the sliding glass doors into the darkness. Silence filled the room except for the off-tune noise of a cicada coming from a palm tree outside, as though it, too, were echoing in agreement to what Jayne had just said. Jayne sighed deeply and patted Shyla's hand, "When the time is right, you will know it, and you will take the initiative to regain control over your life."

After Jayne left Shyla tried calling Carl at home one last time before turning out the light. Her headache had returned. It had been a long day and she was tired. She really didn't feel like talking to him now, especially after finding that paper, but she had told him she would call. On the fifth ring he answered.

Chapter Four

It was a small thing, really, when she thought about it, but one of the things she missed most since marrying Carl was getting up around five o'clock every morning and walking for thirty minutes or so. She loved that time of day. Predawn. It was when things were just beginning to happen, but not quite yet. There was a newness to the scent in the air. She liked listening to the tree frogs as they tuned their deep croaking sounds to the higher-pitched tones of daylight; and to the chirping of birds, at first tentative, but gradually erupting into a cacophony of unorchestrated notes at the sun's breaking. And the sunrise. On the east coast of Florida where Shyla lived, the colors of dawn were deep and bold and usually overstated, but here at Ibis, facing the warm waters of the Gulf, the hues of the horizon were softer somehow, more pastel. The harshness wasn't visible.

Early morning had been Shyla's creative time, that time of day when in her mind outlines were formed, new characters invented, chapters fleshed out, and entire stories written. It had been part of the reason she felt excited with each new day and why she had so much energy. Somehow it had also been connected to her happiness.

Walking around the campus of Ibis on this morning brought all of these feelings that Shyla had lovingly stored away back to full front. Carl didn't like to walk, especially early in the morning. He just couldn't get awake then. And when he did finally wake up, he wanted Shyla there next to him. They had so little time to share together as it was, which made their mornings together even more important. Of course, they usually ate breakfast in bed, something Carl insisted on, delaying the inevitable time when he would finally have to get up and then rush to get ready for work. By that time Shyla was already tired, listless, and filled with anxiety. She didn't even like to eat breakfast, at least not the big breakfast Carl fixed. All she wanted was a small bowl of cereal and a cup of tea. But she forced herself to eat at least some of whatever Carl prepared.

Shyla slowed her pace and took a deep breath. She was starting to feel the anxiety build up inside of her again. A headache wasn't too far off. It was probably because she hadn't walked in a while. Her cottage was the next block over. She would go back and eat a bowl of cereal. Then she would be all right.

When Shyla turned the corner, she was startled to see Mariela sitting in her red sports car parked in front of her cottage. The door was open on the driver's side, and music was playing softly from the car stereo. When Mariela saw Shyla, she turned off the radio and got out of the car holding a folder.

"Mariela, are you all right?"

"I have never been better. Look, I know it's crazy for me to show up like this, especially this time of morning. God, I didn't even know it ever got this early. It's just that I finished that short story I mentioned to you."

Shyla glanced down at the folder Mariela was holding. "It's not crazy at all. I think it is wonderful that you finished it. Come in and I will fix us some tea. I don't have any Cuban coffee, but . . ."

"No, I won't come in now. Thank you anyway. I need to get back to Trégo, and I'll see you in class this afternoon. I just wanted you to have it now. I know you probably have a zillion things to do, but in case you have some free time, I'd appreciate it if you would read it and tell me what you think."

"Of course I will." Shyla reached out and hugged Mariela. "I have never had a child, but I think writing something in which you really feel passionate about is a lot like giving birth."

Mariela didn't say anything. She had known Shyla would understand.

After Mariela left, Shyla went inside her cottage to shower and dress. Then she ate a bowl of cereal and fixed a cup of tea. The feeling of anxiety had passed. Picking up the folder, she carried it and her tea to the sofa. There was still plenty of time before her first class. She took out the manuscript and read,

The Immigrant

There had always been a plan. At first embedded in the embryo, it developed within, from infant to girl, girl to woman; and then passed on. "Like one of those seeds taken out of the Egyptian Pyramids, which, after being three thousand years a seed and nothing but a seed, being planted in English soil, it developed itself, and grew to greenness, . . . "

When the plan finally reached maturity, twenty-three immigrants led by The Guardian began their journey that took them from Cuba to a southern-most point of the mainland. Supplied with a coffin of hemp and seaweed, very little food or water, and the inheritance, the journey continued throughout the remainder of their lives.

Shyla read the manuscript through without stopping. When she finished, she read it again. It was the story of a Santeria priestess escaping Cuba. The sheer power of the words left her weak. The story itself was incredible. In all her years as a writer, she had never come across so much obvious talent. She found it hard to believe that it was Mariela's first serious attempt at creative writing. "My gosh," she said staring at the manuscript pages.

Still holding onto the manuscript, she carried her cup of tea over to the microwave to reheat it. She had been so absorbed in Mariela's story that she had forgotten to drink it. She thought about calling Mariela, but she didn't know what her situation was at the home she called Trégo; it was still early and she didn't want to disturb anyone who might be asleep. It would be better to just wait. Mariela had said she would see Shyla at her afternoon class. She would talk to her then. In the meantime, she would make a phone call to her editor and tell him about Mariela's story. If he liked it, and she was positive he would, she wanted to feel him out on the idea of *The Immigrant* being expanded into a novel.

That afternoon Shyla walked over to the lecture hall in the education building early just in case Mariela was there. She needn't have bothered, because Mariela didn't get there until fifteen minutes after class had started. With so many students signed up for Shyla's course, she ran over the scheduled two hours. Once everyone left, however, she was finally able to sit down at one of the desks and talk to Mariela.

Once she started talking about the story, Shyla couldn't contain her excitement. She remembered the first short story she had written and the euphoria she experienced when she realized that it was good. There was so much she wanted to say to encourage Mariela, but whatever she did, she didn't want to make her think that getting published would be easy. It wasn't.

"Is this story about your own family history, Mariela?"

"I honestly don't know, Shyla. I have always had vivid dreams, even to the extent of sleep-walking and talking. And, of course, I remember stories from my childhood. I guess my imagination just carried it forward a bit. When you said the other day that everyone has a story within them to be written, I think that perhaps this is my story."

Shyla nodded.

"Well, you have a gift, and I hope you will put it to use." Shyla told Mariela about her phone conversation with her editor. "He would be interested in seeing it completed as a novel, if you feel you want to do that."

"Oh, I do. Yes."

"Then that is exactly what you should do."

Shyla took Mariela's hands and held them. She could feel the vibrant energy and enthusiasm surge through them into her own. It seemed as though she was the one making a promise to someone or something to write this story. It was time for it to be told. It was time for it to be born.

* * *

Carl splashed cold water on his face and spread his eyes open with his fingers. The reflection in the mirror confirmed how he felt; he looked like shit. Slowly he began his morning routine of brushing his teeth, shaving, showering, and dressing. He tried to keep from thinking about it, but he couldn't. He had been a complete fool. He never should have taken Andrea to lunch the day before. It was just a game between them. Two people teasing one another, taking it a little further each time, just to see who would back down first. Well, Andrea didn't back down, and he couldn't. She was sexy and she excited him. She was also willing.

He had hoped Shyla wouldn't call last night, but, of course, he knew she would. She had said she would. It had been hard talking to her, thinking of things to say, trying to sound cheerful and normal. Normal. What a joke. He was so keyed up over this Andrea thing that he couldn't even take a decent crap. At one point Shyla had even asked him if he was all right; he sounded tired. That was it. He was just tired. She believed him. Sweet, trusting Shyla.

Then, of course, there had been his mother to face. She must have the nose of a blood hound. She had smelled Andrea's perfume right away. He had to do some fast thinking on that one. Now she was determined to contact Deena and Christine, either with or without his help. She wouldn't be put off any longer. He would try calling his two daughters again later in the day and feel them out, assuming he could get some privacy to use his own phone in his own office. His mother wanted them all to go out to dinner Friday evening. Then, sometime while her sister was still visiting from Argentina, she would invite them over to her house. He didn't know how Shyla was going to take it. He had a feeling she had met just about all of his relatives she wanted to meet. She didn't even know he and his kids were speaking to one another, if you could call it that.

Now he had to go into the office and face Andrea. God he dreaded it. Maybe she would be out sick or something. One thing was for sure, he must never let what happened at lunch the day before happen again. He loved Shyla, and he would never do anything to hurt her. Screwing around with Andrea was purely physical. It meant nothing. Even so, it shouldn't have happened and he must not let it happen again. He would do his work and take Mario to lunch with him. If Mario had plans, he would order take-in and eat it at his desk. He would definitely not take Andrea to lunch any more, or anywhere else for that matter.

Carl finished dressing and started stuffing his pockets with his wallet, some loose change, and the small scraps of paper he normally accumulated from day to day. One of the papers fell to the floor. It was the credit card receipt from yesterday's lunch with Andrea. Two hundred fifty-nine dollars for lunch; the room alone had been close to one hundred eighty dollars. He ripped the receipt into tiny shreds and flushed them down the commode.

* * *

The Board of Directors meeting Jayne had called didn't last as long as Terry thought it would. Basically everyone agreed that some sort of trust needed to be set up in order to protect the principal of the Fanjul donation. Terry would handle that piece. Then, once plans were in place to launch the building campaign which was already being discussed, the Fanjul money would be the catalyst for attracting other sizeable donations. By then, Augusto Fanjul might even drop another chunk of money into the coffer; that is, if his only child was still showing an active interest in writing. There was even mention of naming one of the new buildings after Augusto Fanjul or perhaps Mariela's grandfather, Octavio. Terry smiled at the irony of it. A Cuban-born Hispanic living in the United States who couldn't read let alone write the English language having a building at an elite, high-brow writer's college named after him. Only in America.

Terry fumbled with his car keys trying to unlock the door when he noticed Shyla loaded down with papers coming out of the academic building. Terry watched her drop some of the papers and then, without much success, struggle to pick them up. He rushed over to where she was.

"Well, hello."

Shyla stooped down to keep the satchel from slipping off her shoulder and looked up. "Terry. How nice to see you."

He took the papers from her arms and lifted the satchel from her shoulder, hanging it from his own. "Looks like I got here in the nick of time. Do you plan to read all of these things?"

Shyla laughed. "Yes. I believe it is the only way." The two of them fell into step. "Are you just wandering around looking for damsels in distress or are you actually my guardian angel in disguise?"

Shyla's Initiative

"Jayne invited me to a Board of Directors meeting. It just finished and I was on my way to my car when I saw you."

Shyla could feel him staring at her and glanced at him.

"I'm sorry," he said. "It's just that I don't have a clue as to what color your hair is. The other day at lunch, I could have sworn it was brunette. But this afternoon, with the sun shining on it, it is a mixture of light brown, blond, brunette, and there is even a rose color in it."

"I am afraid my hair has always had a mind of its own. It makes me feel like a chameleon; my hair and eyes change color according to whatever mood I am in."

"No, your eyes are definitely blue." Terry shifted the weight of the papers. "Looks like you have a big group," he said indicating the papers.

"It is," Shyla answered quickly. "I asked everyone to write a fifteen-hundred-word picture book using the animal of their choice as the protagonist. It's a silly assignment, actually, but I have used it before and found it to be revealing. I believe that all writers have their own writer's voice, but often the most difficult part of writing is being able to listen to that voice and express it in writing. Sometimes it is a child's voice, or sometimes it is an adult voice. By writing a picture book with specific guidelines, the students are forced to demonstrate which voice they are listening to and whether it is natural or whether they are forcing it. The plan was that I would read them this afternoon so I could return them by next class period. But I'm not sure I can get them all read; some of the students obviously went over the fifteen-hundred-word limit. I was beginning to wonder if I was even going to make it to my cottage." Shyla smiled at him to show her appreciation.

"By the way, I know you will keep this confidential, but Mariela has written something that I feel is publishable. She is going to try expanding it into a novel. It really is that good."

"I am glad to hear it. That will certainly make her father proud and happy. Mariela, needless to say, has always been sort of a loose end around Trégo. If she finds something to keep her attention, like writing, maybe she will settle down."

They reached Shyla's cottage and Terry put the bag and other papers on the desk by the window. "Well, I guess I'd better get back to the office and do what it is I get paid to do." Terry hesitated by the door. "Shyla, I just want you to know, if you ever need anything, legal or otherwise, I hope you will feel you can come to me. You can trust me."

"I know that," said Shyla. "Thank you."

Terry bent down and kissed her lightly on the cheek. "Happy reading."

Shyla watched him long-stride it across the lawn toward the parking lot. For that one brief moment, she felt a surge of happiness, something she hadn't felt in a long time.

* * *

Mariela felt possessed. She thought of nothing else but *The Immigrant*. The story was already there, complete and wholly contained in her mind; Mariela was simply the implement being used to record it. Her dreams when she slept were more real and defined now; the color in them more vivid. There was an intelligence about them; a purpose. The images lasted longer. She remembered more of the details upon waking. Words and phrases that in the past had made no sense now belonged; and she had a place to put them. Shyla had told her she was good. That was all she needed to know. The voice in her head would now guide her.

One thing Shyla insisted on was that Mariela prepare an outline of her novel and some sketches of all the characters. It would help keep her from going off the main track of the story. The outline didn't have to be comprehensive; just a beginning, a middle, and an ending, with a few major occurrences and situations in between. The sketches could be brief, even lists of things that revealed her characters. Once she had that completed, she could begin writing the first chapter, filling in the spaces, and bringing her story to life. She was anxious to start. Hopefully she could at least have a draft of the first chapter completed by Saturday for Shyla to look at.

The outline proved to be much more difficult than Mariela anticipated. Everything was inside her head, and it only came out chronologically as she was actually writing the story. To leap ahead from the beginning to the middle, or from the middle to the end was like disemboweling an animal. Because she didn't know where her story was going until she actually wrote it, it was difficult for her to see into the development of it. She struggled with it, not even taking time out to go to the main house and eat with her father. As always, RaRa stayed nearby, hovering, attending to her wants and needs, fixing her food and drink, and keeping Mariela's world in the west wing orderly.

The character sketches went more easily. Mariela felt as though she were writing about people she had known intimately all of her life. She could actually visualize them. Names and places seemed to spill from her mind, along with descriptions. There was nothing she didn't know about her characters. They were now a part of her. When she finally completed the outline and sketches, she showered and dressed and drove to Ibis in order to let Shyla read over them. Only after she had Shyla's approval would she actually start writing the first chapter of her story.

Chapter Five

Carl made it to the office in record time. He had already missed a half day from the day before so he really needed to get some work done. Not only that, he wanted to get there before Andrea so that he could call his daughters without Andrea listening in. As luck would have it, no sooner had he parked and flipped open the trunk lid to retrieve his computer bag when Andrea's black BMW pulled into the parking space next to his.

"Hello, lover," she greeted him smiling.

"Hello, yourself." He wanted to sound nonchalant. He stood behind his trunk fiddling with the strap on his bag hoping she would go on inside the building.

"I had a wonderful time yesterday. Thank you." She came over and stood next to him.

"You are quite welcome." The words as well as her perfume gagged him. When it became obvious that she was going to wait for him so they could walk into the building together, he yanked his bag out of the trunk and slammed the trunk lid closed. Several other people were arriving. He noticed a couple of them looking their way. The gossip mills would soon be running rampant, no doubt.

During the course of the morning Carl called the number where his older daughter worked three times, each time when Andrea had gone out of the office. All three times whoever answered the phone told him that Deena couldn't come to the phone. Would he like to leave a message? He waited until right before lunch and dialed again. This time Deena answered the phone herself.

"I thought it was going to take an act of Congress to get to talk to you today," he said laughing. "How is everything?"

"Busy."

"I gathered that much. So, what's new?"

"Nothing. Look, do you want something?"

This obviously wasn't a good time to reveal to his daughter that the grandmother she hadn't seen or spoken to since she was ten years old now wanted to kiss and make up. Of course, knowing Deena, there probably would never be a good time. "All right, I'll make this quick. Your grandmother has moved down from New Jersey and is living here in West Palm Beach now. She wants to see you and Christine."

There was nothing but silence on the other end of the line. Carl couldn't even hear his daughter breathing. "Deena? Did you hear me?"

"Is this some kind of stupid joke?"

"No, it isn't. In fact, I was hoping all of us could meet somewhere nice for dinner tomorrow night and just sort of get to know each other again." Carl was trying to keep calm. Deena had her mother's smart-aleck mouth and it infuriated him whenever she talked disrespectfully to him.

"All of us?"

"Well, Shyla won't be with us; she's teaching a writing course in Naples. But your grandmother, you and Christine, and me."

"I already have plans."

Carl's anger thermometer had already gone as high as it could. He hated groveling, especially to his own daughter. She had the upper hand, and she knew it.

"Listen, it doesn't matter to me whether you make up with your grandmother or not, but it matters to her. Just have dinner with her tomorrow night. After that, it will be entirely up to you whether you ever see her again."

Deena didn't answer. Finally she said, "I was planning on working late tomorrow night for the overtime so I can get my car fixed."

Carl knew he was being manipulated, but he wanted to get this thing scheduled once and for all. "How much is it going to cost to get your car fixed?"

"Five hundred dollars."

Carl sucked in his breath. There wasn't that much money in the checking account, and he still didn't know how in the hell he was going to pay for the bill he ran up yesterday at Four Seasons. "O.K. I'll loan you the money, and you can pay me back whenever you get it. How does that sound?" He would get a cash advance on his credit card.

"I'll think about it."

"Well, let me know something by tonight so I can make the reservations. OK?"

The line went dead. Deena had hung up.

At least she was going to consider it. Carl ripped the piece of paper he had been scribbling on from the pad and threw it in the trash can. Then he dialed his other daughter's number. There was no answer. He had been trying to call her on and off for days, but hadn't been able to reach her. Maybe Deena would know where she was and tell her. For now, that was all he could do. Besides, Andrea had come back into the office.

Chapter Six

The next morning Terry finished running off the last of the copies of the documents that would be sent to the Ibis Board members. First, though, he wanted Jayne to read over everything to make sure it was to her liking. As far as he was concerned, Jayne was Ibis, and it was what she wanted that mattered.

He glanced at the clock on his desk. Shyla's morning class finished up around 11:45. If he hurried, he might be able to catch her. Her next class didn't start until two o'clock, so maybe she would let him take her off-campus somewhere for lunch. There was a pretty little place, sort of rustic, down on the wharf that he hadn't been to in a while. It had a nice view of the Gulf and was the kind of place that needed to be enjoyed with someone.

"I won't be back until late," Terry told his secretary and then walked out the door whistling.

Terry parked in front of the administration building and dropped off the documents with Mrs. Fowler explaining that he would call Jayne about them later. Then he got in his car and drove it to Shyla's cottage just in case she had finished up early. When she didn't come to the door, he began walking across the large expanse of lawn known as "the common" toward the lecture hall. She was just coming out of the building, loaded down, as usual, with manuscripts.

She laughed when she saw him walking towards her. "I knew it. You are my guardian angel."

"I only wish I could be so lucky," he answered taking all of the papers from her and tucking them under one arm. "The real reason I am here is because it's Friday, it's a beautiful day, much too nice to be stuck in the office or a classroom, and I was hoping you would let me take you to lunch. There's a place I especially like, nothing fancy, but the food is good, and we can sit outside. That way we can enjoy some of this nice weather we're having." He noticed her looking away. "I promise to have you back in plenty of time for your next class," he encouraged.

Shyla didn't say anything, and Terry was starting to feel embarrassed and even a little alarmed. Maybe he had overstepped his bounds. "If this is a bad time or you're too busy or something." He jammed his free hand into the pocket of his trousers. "It's just that I like this place, but I really don't enjoy going there by myself."

Shyla looked up at him and smiled. "I don't feel like eating on campus today either. I think it is a wonderful idea. Thank you for asking."

After dropping off the manuscripts at Shyla's cottage, they got in Terry's car and headed west toward the ocean highway. Fifteen minutes later they arrived at what Shyla thought looked like a fish camp. Everything was wood, roughly thrown together, unpainted, and covered in barnacles if it was in water. Inside, all of the walls had paintings and other artwork, most of it folk art, hanging from them, and outside on the deck pelicans and seagulls perched on nearby pilings. Terry led Shyla to an empty table on the deck and they sat down.

Shyla absolutely loved it. The sound of the water lapping against the wooden pilings, the mournful cries of water fowl, and the occasional honk of a passing boat. It was peaceful and relaxing, as though they had stepped into another world.

"Do you like it?" Terry asked, but he already knew her answer. She hadn't stopped smiling since they first arrived.

Terry stretched out his long athletic legs and then awkwardly reeled them back in, crossing them somewhere between his ankles and knees and then somehow stuffed them under the chair where he was sitting. A waitress making the rounds between the tables glanced at Terry appreciatively. She was a young college student, probably half his age, but Terry was one of the lucky ones who either through quality genetics or healthy living had managed to retain his good looks.

"And what can I get for you two here?" the waitress asked.

"Would you like a glass of wine?" Terry asked.

"Yes, I'll have a glass of Chardonnay, please."

"Make that two," Terry added. "We'll order later." The waitress scribbled on her notepad, left, and in a few minutes returned with the wine.

"Here's to special friendships," said Terry holding up his glass.

"Special friendships," Shyla repeated and sipped her wine.

Terry studied her as she sat quietly watching a small skiff bob not too far from the shoreline and eventually make its way into the deeper waters. Never had anyone held so much fascination for him. He knew part of the reason was that even though they had just met, he felt he already knew her, mainly because he knew her writing. Another thing that fascinated him about her was even as private as she was, he had never met anyone with such revealing, expressive eyes. She was completely vulnerable, and she didn't even know it.

Shyla said something about the skiff, and Terry suddenly realized that he had been staring at her. "I now know the color of your hair," he said somewhat embarrassed when Shyla looked at him. "It's fawn."

Shyla laughed and took another sip of wine. "Well, I am so relieved to have that question answered," she said teasing him. "I won't have to worry about that one any more. I'll just scratch it right off my list."

There was so much Terry wanted to ask Shyla, but he didn't dare. The ball was in her court; if she wanted him to know anything, she would tell him. Better to keep things neutral and impersonal. "Are you enjoying your classes at Ibis this year?"

"Very much. I get so much out of them. Every year there is a new surprise for me—a new talent, a new friend."

Mariela was a new talent. He wondered if he could be the new friend.

"What about your own writing? Are you working on anything now?" Terry noticed a shadow pass over Shyla's face and immediately regretted asking about her writing. "I'm sorry, Shyla. You must overlook my inquisitiveness and stupidity. It's just that you are the first author I have ever known, and I don't know what the limits are as far as what I should or should not ask when it comes to your work."

"You can ask anything you want. There are no limits. It's just that right now, my writing is a rather sore subject with me. I can't even write a grocery list, much less something to send to my editor."

Terry nodded. "Isn't this kind of a normal thing to happen to writers, though? I mean, writer's block and all of that?"

"To other writers, maybe. Not to me. I have always had the problem of having too many ideas and not enough time to write them all down. As I was finishing one manuscript, I would already be thinking about the next project I wanted to write."

"I am sure it is just temporary, then. Probably a couple of weeks away from your writing, and then you will be back with more ideas than ever."

"It's already been eight months," Shyla said softly.

Terry felt the pain he saw in Shyla's face. "What happened eight months ago?" he asked.

"I got married."

Terry looked away. Of course he had known she was married; Jayne had told him. And he knew that she had remarried after being a widow for several years. "I have never been married," said Terry. "I came close one time, but . . ."

"No cigar?" offered Shyla.

"That's right," he said smiling. "Marriage is such a deep commitment, it seems to me. A few words are spoken, vows are made, and all of a sudden your mind, your body, and everything that you are is supposed to be shared with someone else. If it isn't the right someone else, then everything gets eschewed and thrown off-center." He glanced toward the skiff. It was bobbing its way back to shore. "In all of the divorce cases I have handled, the one thing that is consistently lacking between the husband and wife is trust. Without that as the foundation, the marriage doesn't stand a chance, or so it seems."

Just then the waitress came back to take their order. Shyla ordered a shrimp salad plate, and Terry ordered fish and chips. When the waitress left, Shyla didn't pick up the conversation where they had left off, and Terry knew it was best if he didn't. Instead they talked about Shyla's students and what they had been writing and about some of the more interesting cases Terry had handled.

They stayed longer than they had intended, and Terry had to hurry to get Shyla back so she wouldn't be late for her class. She told him it had been a wonderful afternoon and one she would always remember. Her eyes said the same thing.

* * *

Just about everyone had already left the building to go home including Andrea, who had left early. Carl had stayed, hoping Deena would call. He hadn't even taken a break to go to the bathroom, afraid that she would call while he was away from his desk, get discouraged, and then not call back. Now, after three cups of coffee, he had to take a leak, and it wouldn't wait until he got home. He got up from his desk and headed for the men's room. When he returned a few minutes later, the blinking light on his phone indicated there was a message. In was from Deena. She wouldn't be able to meet them on Friday evening, but she could have lunch with them on Saturday. Noon, at the Olive Garden. She and Christine would come together.

Carl did some quick scheduling in his mind. Saturday morning he had to pick up his mother no later than four o'clock in order to get to the airport in Miami in time to meet the plane her sister would be arriving on. Assuming the flight was on time, and taking into account he would have to get the luggage, go through customs, and maybe push a wheelchair with his mother in it if her arthritis was acting up, they could get back to his mother's in plenty of time for him to unload everything and then take them to lunch at the Olive Garden. He personally wouldn't have chosen the Olive Garden. He knew his mother expected something a little more elegant with a white tablecloth, flowers and candles on the table, and good Spanish cooking. But this was good enough. At least he was getting his kids and his mother together. It shouldn't matter that Aunt Rosa would be there too. He could go to Ana's later that afternoon and do whatever needed to be done to the pool.

He snatched up the phone and dialed his mother's telephone number so he could tell her, not wanting to wait until he saw her when he stopped by her place in a short while for supper. He hoped that she would be pleased.

* * *

Pilar sat in her recliner by the window in the living room with the phone pressed against her ear, looking through the verticals, and occasionally shrugging. For several minutes she said nothing. Finally she grunted into the mouthpiece. What Carlos told her wasn't what she had wanted at all. To begin with, it would be awkward, to say the least, with her sister there watching everything take place. Pilar didn't know how her grandchildren would behave around her. If they were unpleasant, Rosa would see it and waste no time in reporting it to all the other family members. Carlos had told her that they were looking forward to meeting her again, and that Deena had even suggested the Olive Garden because she thought her grandmother would enjoy it. That was another thing. The Olive Garden was just a notch above fast food as far as Pilar was concerned. Not only that, it was Italian, not Spanish. How could the child possibly think she would like it. She grunted again into the phone.

"Listen, Mother, Deena and Christine are both very busy with their jobs and all. This is the only time they could both get together. It is either Saturday for lunch, or not at all." Carl was getting furious. Why did this always happen? He was caught right in the middle of something that he didn't want any part of. His mother had always been that way. Looking back on it, that was the main reason they had had their disagreement in the first place. She was like a twenty-legged octopus, always reaching another tentacle out, pulling him in and sucking the life out of him. She was so needy; nothing ever pleased her, it seemed, no matter what he did or how hard he tried. He took a deep breath and tried to relax. "It will be nice," he said.

Pilar finally went along with it, but she didn't like it. At least Shyla wasn't going to be there. Carlos always fussed so much over her whenever she was around. Maybe she could tell Rosa that Deena and Christine planned everything in order to meet her when they found out she was coming all the way from Argentina. Rosa would like that. It would make her think she was the one getting all of the attention, as usual.

* * *

Maria wouldn't sleep for the next twenty-four hours. It was part of the cleansing and purification necessary for the ceremony. The preparations for *ébo* were in place. As the high priestess, now she would begin the ritual of *lyalochas*, just as it had been passed down orally to her from her mother, her mother's mother, and before that.

She stood in front of the small mirror in her bedroom to which had been attached the gifts she had offered venerating the *orishas*. Below the mirror, on a white linen cloth, lay her necklaces, the *ilekes*, which were the sacred banners of the *orishas* themselves. One by one she picked up each necklace, kissing it before putting it on: *Eleggua*, red and black, messenger between human beings and the other *orishas*, the first to be honored; *Obatala*, white, the *orisha* of peace and harmony; *Yemayá*, blue and white, protector of women; *Shangó*, the thunder god to give power over others, red and white; and *Oshún*, yellow and amber, the goddess of love and beauty. Each of the deities would be petitioned. Now there was only *ébo*. There was nothing else left for them to do: Maria, Miguel, Juan, and Jesus. She gazed at her reflection in the mirror. All of the *ilekes* were in place around her neck, each colored bead a symbol. Somewhere in the distance, coming from beyond the courtyard in the direction of the cypress grove, the beating of the drum continued, now a little harder, a little faster.

* * *

Normally, Friday class attendance was small, with many of the students leaving early in an attempt to enjoy the weather and take a long weekend. Shyla didn't have that many manuscripts to go over, and after getting back from lunch with Terry, she decided it would be a good idea to go home the next morning—even if it was just for one night. After all, there were no Saturday or Sunday classes scheduled. She told Jayne of her plans just before her afternoon session started. Jayne invited her for an early supper that evening, and then Shyla would drive to West Palm early Saturday morning.

What Terry had said made sense. Without trust in a marriage, nothing else worked. That was why she had been so anxious and unable to write. She had changed her whole life around to suit the needs of Carl and his mother, but, in all fairness, he hadn't asked her to. She simply did it. She needed to refocus on what was important to her; namely, her writing. If she told Carl how she honestly felt and explained what kinds of things were causing her to be distrustful, then maybe he would understand. After all, he loved her, and she loved him. She was sure they could work it out. They just needed to open up to each other a little more, especially where his mother was concerned.

When she got to her cottage she settled down to go over the latest batch of stories her students had turned in. She had asked them to write a romance short story using two restrictions: There had to be a happy ending, and the story had to engage the emotions of the reader. Hopefully, she would be able to finish with them that evening. Then she could leave for West Palm Beach right after breakfast the next morning.

* * *

Before picking up Shyla for their early dinner, Jayne called Terry at his office to thank him for getting all of the documents prepared so quickly.

"Glad to do it. If there is anything you have a question about or you don't like, just let me know and I will fix it."

Jayne talked about some of the things she was considering in order to improve Ibis, in addition to the building expansion, one of them being to bring in major authors from all over the world to participate in the summer retreat. She also mentioned in the conversation that she had seen Shyla after lunch and that Shyla had decided to drive home on Saturday since there were no classes scheduled. She would return Sunday afternoon.

After Jayne hung up she couldn't help but feel she had said something to upset Terry. She couldn't imagine what. Maybe he was just tired. He had, after all, spent a lot of time getting everything prepared for the next Board meeting. That was probably it.

Jayne took Shyla to a sports bar and grill located just off campus. She was a little concerned about Shyla driving on Alligator Alley over the weekend to and from West Palm Beach. Normally, that was when the large farm trucks loaded with oranges, cane, and corn were either entering or exiting the highway, making traffic a nightmare, not to mention all of the road construction taking place. Shyla assured her she would be all right. "I had better talk to him while I am in this mood," said Shyla when she explained her reason for wanting to go. "If I wait, I might chicken out." Jayne understood. It couldn't be easy to explain to the man you were married to that his mother was a pain in the ass and that he was allowing her as well as all the rest of the baggage he was dragging along to destroy their marriage. She had been through her own relationship problems with George. In fact, that was the main reason she never married him. Just living together seemed to work better—at least where she was concerned.

After eating, Jayne went home, leaving Shyla to finish going over the papers from her afternoon class. By ten o'clock Shyla was exhausted and she still wasn't finished. Carl had said he would call when she talked to him the night before, but he hadn't. She got ready for bed, thinking she would feel better if she finished the few remaining manuscripts the next morning before she left.

Chapter Seven

Carl's blood pressure shot up about twenty notches when the alarm on the clock radio went off. He couldn't believe it was time to get up already. After he had eaten dinner with his mother the night before, she had wanted him to finish hanging the verticals in the dining room and spare bedroom so that the house would look nice while her sister was visiting. It wasn't a difficult job, but it had taken him longer than it should have, mainly because his mother kept getting in the way, interrupting him with questions about Deena and Christine. He finally got home around 11:30, too late to call Shyla he told himself.

He slung his legs over the side of the bed and yanked up the phone. His mother had asked him to call her when he got up just to make sure she didn't over-sleep. She wasn't used to getting up so early and she didn't want to be late in picking up her sister at the airport. After he called her, he quickly showered and dressed. His mother was standing outside on the sidewalk waiting for him when he got there. It was still dark.

They arrived at the airport fifteen minutes before the plane was to arrive. By the time they found the correct gate where the passengers would be coming in, the plane had landed. It was on time.

Going through customs took longer than Carl had expected, but eventually his Aunt Rosa was cleared through and all he had to do was load into the car everything and everyone. Everyone meant not only his mother and Aunt Rosa, but his cousin, KiKi, and her two young children as well. They had decided to make the trip at the last minute. They would be visiting Pilar only a couple of days, and then they were going on to Orlando to see Disney World. Of course Aunt Rosa would be staying behind with Pilar.

It took quite a bit of shuffling around to get all of the luggage squeezed into the car. Finally, with the kids sitting on laps and a couple of smaller suitcases wedged into the backseat, they were ready to make the two-hour drive to West Palm Beach.

The sheer volume of voices in the car, all speaking at once in Spanish, made it difficult for Carl to concentrate on the tricky turns necessary to get out of the maze of airport roads and back on the interstate. Twice he had to turn around and head back. Eventually he got it right, but it was cutting it close if they were going to make it to the restaurant by noon.

"Carlos, I don't have enough room for everyone to stay." His mother, sitting next to him in the front seat, had momentarily stopped yelling at everyone in the backseat and now focused her attention on him. Her condo had just one extra bedroom with a single bed. "Maybe they," meaning the cousin and the two kids, "can stay at your house. It will only be for two nights and then they will leave." When Carl didn't say anything, she added, "Of course, Rosa and I can stay there too, for that matter. That way everyone can visit. I will do all the cooking and you won't have to worry about driving everyone back and forth to my house so much."

It was going to be a mess no matter what he decided. If they all crammed into his mother's place, she would never let him live it down. If only his cousin and her kids stayed at his house and his aunt stayed at his mother's, he would be spending every waking hour hauling them back and forth to see one another. At least if they all stayed together at his house, they could visit and he wouldn't have to take so much time off from work. By the time Shyla got back in town, everyone would be gone except for Rosa, and she would be staying at his mother's place by then. In the end that is what they agreed to, and at quarter to twelve, he pulled into the driveway, unlocked the front door, and quickly unloaded all the suitcases and assortment of bags, leaving everything in the living room temporarily. Of course, everyone had to go to the bathroom; but, as Pilar quickly pointed out, there were three bathrooms in the house, and she took it upon herself to show everyone where each one was located.

* * *

By late morning Shyla was on her way, once again navigating Alligator Alley, only this time headed east for West Palm Beach. The number of trucks on the highway was incredible, and the brightness from the rising sun made driving difficult. She smiled thinking about what Mariela had told her in that little road-side cafe. "I bet you could speed up to at least 35 or 40 miles an hour if you wanted to," she had told her. Not in this traffic, Shyla muttered to herself.

She was a little apprehensive about the things she wanted to discuss with Carl, but she knew it was the right thing to do. Being married meant sharing everything. It was only fair to Carl that she share her concerns so he would at least know how she felt and why. Who knows. Maybe he had been having some of the same concerns, but was afraid to say anything to Shyla. This would be a positive thing. Once they were able to get this resolved with some new ground rules that now involved Pilar, there was no reason why her relationship with Pilar couldn't be improved as well.

The closer she got to West Palm, the happier she started to feel. She thought of all the good times she and Carl had shared before they got married. There had been so much laughter then and so much love between them. How could she have let that slip away just because his mother had moved nearby? Somehow she had lost her own identify when she lost the trust she had placed in Carl. Now she was going to prove to him that he still had her trust by being totally honest with him. After all, he hadn't actually done anything to make her doubt him. He was just a considerate son. That is probably what made him a considerate husband as well. She just needed to have some reassurance that it was their relationship that came first because it was the most important thing. If he believed that, everything else would fall into place.

It was already past noon when she reached the outskirts of West Palm Beach. It would take her another hour to drive through the city to the small residential community where she lived. She thought about stopping and calling him at the house to let him know she was coming, but then decided she would rather surprise him. He would probably be out in the yard anyway mowing the grass or pruning the hedges; he wouldn't be able to hear the telephone ring.

***

Terry had some errands to run and while out decided to drive over to Ibis and see if anything was going on. Of course he knew there weren't any classes scheduled, but it was a nice, warm day to take a short drive. After dropping off his laundry and picking up a few groceries, he followed the shoreline drive south until he reached the Ibis entrance. The guard at the gate recognized him, smiled, and waved him on through.

It was a beautiful campus. Since Jayne had been named president, not once in all that time could Terry remember a single negative incident to occur at Ibis. Jayne ran a tight ship. She was intelligent, professional, and she was not the type to fall for any bull shit. Now with this large donation from the Fanjul family, she would be able to realize some of her own dreams of how she wanted to see Ibis progress. Terry was happy for her.

He drove around the administrative building and past the lecture hall and cafeteria. Then he turned toward the cottages, following the black-top road all the way to the end where Hemingway Cottage was located. He knew Shyla's car wouldn't be there. In fact, there were very few cars on campus, mostly those owned by the maintenance personnel and security.

Feeling somewhat let down, Terry drove back out the gate and headed toward town. Maybe it was for the best. Certainly, open lines of communication were essential in any good relationship. If Shyla could talk to her husband and reach an understanding, then Terry would support her in any way he could. It was her life, after all, her happiness that was at stake here, and her decision. He just hoped she was making the right one.

Once in town, he decided to stop at his office just long enough to see if there were any messages. Terry's office was an old Greek Revival home built at the turn of the century and located in what was now considered the historical district of Naples. He had bought the old place and restored it when he decided to open his own practice. The two-story dwelling situated on a good-sized lot overlooking the Gulf Bay was actually smaller than it looked. The space, however, was comfortable and ideal for his professional needs. There was a nice reception area, and he had made a large conference room where the dining room had once been. The rooms upstairs allowed him to keep his office machines and files separate from his large front office and that of his secretary's, therefore giving the downstairs a homey Southern quality while, at the same time, being functional. The large live oaks draped with Spanish moss that dotted the lawn added to the history and beauty of the place as well. It reminded him somewhat of his boyhood home in Little River where he had grown up.

Getting out of his car, he noticed someone standing on the front porch. Being Saturday, the office was closed, of course, and he knew he hadn't made any appointments. As he got closer, he recognized the man as someone who on occasion had brought things from The Guardian for him to keep. The man's name was Miguel.

"Hello, Miguel, I hope you haven't been waiting long."

Without saying anything, Miguel handed Terry a large brown envelope.

"I will put it with the others, in a safe place," Terry said, taking the envelope.

Miguel nodded and left.

Terry unlocked the front door and went into his office. His secretary had left some yellow sticky notes on his phone so he wouldn't miss them. None of the messages were from Shyla. Still holding the brown envelope he sat down at his desk and stared at it. Just like the others, he had no idea what it contained. Before, he had simply locked them away in the vault until which time The Guardian would tell him otherwise. Miguel had given the last envelope to him the day that Mariela's mother died.

He turned it over and looked at the back. There was clear tape holding the clasp down. Picking up a letter opener, he slit the tape and opened the flap. Inside were several pages of a hand-written document. It appeared to be a will of sorts of someone whose name he didn't recognize. He pulled out the papers and began looking through them. He had taken a couple of semesters of Spanish in college so he would at least half-way understand it when he needed to. But this seemed to be written in an older style of Spanish. There were words and phrases that just didn't quite make sense. Some of it didn't look like Spanish at all. He did manage to pick out the fact that there was a lot of description of the Fanjul properties—the cane fields, the sugar processing plants, the forests, and, of course, Trégo. There also appeared to be a detailed account of how the land was originally acquired, and the mention of several other names, all Hispanic, he didn't recognize. Toward the end of the document there was one name he did recognize, however. Terry dropped the letter opener. "What in the hell is going on?" he said. He flipped back to the first page and tried reading through the document again but without much success. If what he remembered from his freshman college Spanish was even close to being correct, however, as the legal and rightful owner of the Fanjul fortune, it was Maria Santiago Fanjul's wish to leave everything to Shyla Wishon.

Terry retrieved the other envelopes from the vault and opened them. In each envelope there appeared to be the identical document, with only the name of the beneficiary changed. Jayne had mentioned to him once that she had studied archaic and extinct languages, including the ancient Castilian dialect, if that is what this was. He grabbed all of the documents and put them in a briefcase. He didn't know how ethical it was to expose the documents to someone else, but at this point he didn't particularly care. Something he didn't understand was going on at Trégo, and whether she knew it or not, Shyla was somehow involved.

* * *

Mariela hadn't stopped writing since getting home the night before from showing Shyla her outline and character sketches of *The Immigrant*. Shyla had told her she had done a terrific job. All that was left for her to do now was to write her novel. And that was what she was doing. She had no awareness of anything but the computer screen in front of her as she keyed in her story. At some point, in the early hours of the morning, she realized someone had brought in a tray with food on it. Probably RaRa. There was also a pot of hot Cuban coffee. Mariela poured the strong black liquid into a cup and lifted the cover from a plate, removing only a thick piece of crusty bread and eating that. Still she continued to write. She felt no consciousness of time, space, or reality; she had no thought of what was happening around her. She neither heard the drum nor saw RaRa. There was just *The Immigrant*.

For days the small vessel drifted aimlessly in the blistering heat, suspended in a watery balance between retreat and advance. But The Guardian and her followers held fast to their belief that the orishas *would guide and protect them. Then, fourteen days after the journey began, a gentle breeze, at first hardly perceptible, began to lick at the calm seas; tentative at first, and then quickening. The clouds above grew ominous, thick and dark. Angry purple peaks replaced the gentle white caps of the sea, and within moments an unrelenting, drenching rain pounded the boat and the helpless voyagers.*

Doubt surfaced among some of the believers where before there had been no doubt. Their sense of purpose became distorted by confusion and fear. The Guardian, as Iyalocha, *petitioned the* orishas *to watch over the believers and to deliver them safely to the freedom they so desperately sought. Offerings were made. Then, as quickly as it came, the storm subsided, leaving in its wake a gentle northwest breeze to carry the vessel toward its destination. The number of journeymen was fewer now, but those who had survived remained unshaken in their belief in The Guardian—a belief so strong and powerful that not even in death would it be denied.*

* * *

Maria entered the area that encircled the altar. Except for the scattering of white beads mixed in with the colored ones, she was dressed in black, a practice that she had brought with her years earlier from Cuba in an attempt to conceal her role as *Iyalocha* and thus ensure her safety. Even with the passage of time, and under the protection of another government and another country, the fear of discovery survived; old practices were continued.

Juan and Jesus had performed well; the many offerings were in place. Fruits, vegetables, and prepared foods, as well as containers of *chequete*, a drink made from sour orange juice, molasses, corn meal and coconut milk. In a position above the altar were the images of Christ and St. Barbara. This was their special seat of honor. This was where they belonged for *ébo*. Soon Miguel would return. He would bring the sacrificial animal.

Chapter Eight

It was fifteen minutes past noon when Carl drove into the parking lot at Olive Garden. Not bad considering everything. He herded everyone into the restaurant and looked around for Deena and Christine, but didn't see them. It took a few moments for the waitress to find a table not only suitable but big enough for all of them. Finally, after a lot of discussion from his mother, his aunt, and his cousin, they got seated. Only the two kids, Amy and Alberto, who were now starting to feel the effects of the eight-and-a-half-hour flight from Buenos Aires to Miami, didn't seem to care where they sat. A few minutes later Deena and Christine arrived, which precipitated another loud discussion concerning the seating arrangements. Neither Deena nor Christine wanted to sit next to someone they didn't know, and they certainly didn't want to sit next to Pilar. Another chair was moved up to the table, Deena sat next to her dad, Christine sat next to her sister, and the empty chair was placed on the other side of Christine.

Conversation was difficult. Both girls, even though they were of Hispanic origin, had been born in the United States and understood very little Spanish. Rosa, KiKi, and the two kids spoke nothing but Spanish. Carl, since he spoke both languages, made a heroic attempt to translate everything that was spoken, while his mother simply sat glowering and saying nothing. It wasn't the happiest of reunions.

After eating, Carl invited his daughters to join them back at the house. Maybe things would be more relaxed there. They agreed, but only because they were curious to see where their dad was now living. Meanwhile Pilar wanted Carl to take her by her condo so she could pick up a few things along with her car to have at Carl's house since she would be staying there for the next couple of days. Carl would have preferred to do it later. His mother wouldn't be needing anything right away, and not only that, he knew she would still want him to haul her to wherever she wanted to go, whether she had her car or not. But it would be useless to argue with her. It was just easier to do what she wanted.

Deena and Christine were parked in the middle of the driveway waiting when Carl finally got back to the house with everybody. He immediately began carrying luggage and bags to the different spare bedrooms while everyone else wandered from room to room examining everything. The phone rang just as Carl heaved the last suitcase up onto a bed in one of the spare guest rooms. It was Andrea.

"What's wrong?"

"Can you come to the office?"

She sounded like she was crying. "Andrea, this is sort of a bad time . . ."

"I don't have anyone else I can talk to. I've been fired. Please, Carl."

Carl listened to the loud voices moving from the downstairs to the upstairs rooms. They could get settled without him for an hour or so. Also, it would give his mother a chance to talk to Deena and Christine without his being there.

"OK. Give me fifteen minutes."

* * *

Jayne was on her hands and knees grubbing around in her flower beds when Terry arrived. She was surprised to see him. She could tell something had him in full tilt by the way he jumped from his car and long-legged it over to where she was working.

"I need your help, Jayne," he said.

"Of course, anything," said Jayne standing up and stripping off her gloves. "What is it?"

"I need you to promise that you will not tell anyone about what I am going to show you. It could mean a serious breach of ethics on my part for even discussing it with another person, but, at this point, although I'm not sure, it might put Shyla in danger."

Jayne glanced at the briefcase Terry was holding. "Let's go into the house where we can talk."

Jayne examined the documents spread out in front of her on the kitchen table shaking her head. "I didn't even realize there was anyone who still used this dialect," she said. "This is incredible. It is known as *Gaunche* and it has been extinct since the sixteenth century. It is believed to have Afro-Asiatic origins." She glanced up at him. "It isn't even classified now."

Terry looked on as she followed her finger down each page of each document. Then she got to Shyla's name. "My god."

Terry leaned back in the chair and stretched out his long legs. He had been right.

"Well, each document is basically the same, identical will of someone named Maria Santiago Fanjul. The earliest dated document left the Fanjul fortune to Mariela's mother, Octavia Maria Santiago Fanjul. Apparently, just before her death, a new will was prepared naming Mariela sole beneficiary. And now, this most recent will names Shyla." Jayne stared at Terry. "I don't think she even knows the Fanjul family, other than Mariela, of course. And she only just recently met her. What does this mean, Terry?"

"I don't know. I honestly don't know. I am getting some bad vibes about it, though. I think we ought to call Shyla."

Jayne pulled her address book from the top drawer in her desk and looked up Shyla's telephone number in West Palm Beach. Someone with a thick, heavy Spanish accent told her that Shyla was out of town. Before Jayne could say anything else, the person hung up.

"She must not be there yet," she said wondering about all of the background noise she had heard at Shyla's house. "I'll try again later."

Terry nodded. "I need to get back," he said gathering up the papers. "Call me if you talk to her. I'll be at home."

Jayne walked him to his car. "I don't mind telling you, this has me more than a little worried. I guess the thing I don't understand is, who is this Maria Santiago Fanjul? I thought Mariela's father, Augusto, was the heir and rightful owner of everything."

Terry's concern was obvious. "I'll get to the bottom of it—one way or another."

* * *

Someone must be having a big party, was Shyla's first thought when she turned into her neighborhood, the rhythmic salsa beat of Latin music was so loud. Then she noticed a car she didn't recognize parked in the middle of her driveway. She had to drive over the grass in order to get around it. She pushed the automatic opener to raise the garage door. Another car was parked where she normally parked, and it wasn't Carl's. It belonged to Pilar. Leaving her car where it was she got out and went into the house through the back door from the garage.

Inside the house, the noise was almost deafening. Two young children were thrashing one another in the middle of the family room while some woman, presumably their mother, yelled at them in Spanish. The woman barely noticed Shyla.

Shyla went into the living room and could hear other voices and laughter coming from her bedroom. There she saw a young woman going through her jewelry box and someone else holding up one of her bras. When they saw Shyla, they stopped laughing.

Pilar and another elderly woman were just coming down the stairs when Shyla went back into the living room.

"Shyla, why are you home?" Pilar asked and then shrugged.

Shyla could hardly hear her over the noise. "I live here," she said, too stunned to say anything else. She went back into the family room and turned off the compact disc player. There, on the floor, was her great grandmother's china clock. It was broken.

"This is Carlos' family," Pilar's expression of annoyance was replaced with a smile. "They just arrived from Argentina." She began introducing all of the people who until now had said nothing. "These are Carlos' daughters, Deena and Christine." She motioned toward the two young women coming out of Shyla's bedroom, now completely sober.

"Where is Carl?" Shyla finally asked, struggling to be heard over the screams still coming from the two kids.

"He had to go to a meeting." Pilar's smile was now becoming strained. "We were going to stay at your beautiful house since you have so much room, but only for a little while, a few days maybe."

"Where did Carl go for his meeting?" Shyla asked, ignoring Pilar's last comment.

"At his office, I think," then turning to the others, they all immediately broke into an explosion of conversation, none of which Shyla could understand.

Shyla had no trouble backing out of her driveway. At some point in all of the chaos, Carl's two daughters had left in the car that had been blocking Shyla from entering the garage. Shyla felt like her head was ready to explode. She had so much anxiety, her entire body was trembling. She felt a slight spinning sensation. Carl would have an explanation, she kept repeating to herself. It was all just a misunderstanding. There were some nice hotels in the area where his family could stay. He surely didn't plan on everyone staying at her house, knowing how she felt about her home and her privacy. He would take care of it.

All of her life Shyla had been able to turn to her inner-most self, an intensely personal place, at the time of crisis. She thought of it as her quiet center of being. It was where she could work out problems and reach some level of rejuvenation. She felt protected there. She went there now, breathing deeply, and trying desperately to think. It was all just a misunderstanding, she repeated.

His car was easy to spot since there was only his car and one other parked in the lot adjoining the office building. After trying the front door and finding it locked, she went around to the side entrance that she knew Carl frequently used after hours and on weekends when he had to work. His office was located at the end of a long hall and she could hear him talking to someone. When she got there she stopped at the doorway, unable to move, unable to breathe. There was a woman sitting on the edge of Carl's desk. He was standing in front of her, kissing her. Her bare legs were wrapped around his waist, her panties—white with black lace—on a chair across the room. Shyla couldn't see where his hands were.

Shyla's purse which she had been carrying slipped from her hand and dropped to the floor. When Carl heard it he quickly glanced around, backed away and zipped his pants while Andrea rearranged her clothing.

"Shyla, what are you doing here?" He walked toward her smiling with his arms reaching out.

Shyla remained frozen while he wrapped his arms around her and kissed her. "Honey, I don't think you have met Andrea Ramos. She's my office mate. Or was. Unfortunately, she just got some bad news, she's been fired, and I was trying to comfort her."

"Hello, Shyla. I've heard a lot about you." Without looking at her, Andrea picked up her panties and something else from her desk and added them to the stuff she had already packed into a cardboard box. "Well, I think I had better get going. It's nice meeting you." She picked up the box and walked toward the door. Still Shyla didn't move.

Carl leaned down and picked up Shyla's purse and gently guided her into his office.

"Don't be a stranger," Andrea said to Carl arching her eyebrows, and then she left.

Shyla heard each step as Andrea walked the length of the carpeted hallway to the exit. She heard her shift the cardboard box in her arms as she opened the side door. She heard the gravel crunch outside the door as she walked on the path leading away from the building, and then the door slowly close. She didn't hear Carl tell her how glad he was to see her, and how beautiful she was, and how much he loved her.

Somehow she managed to leave the building and drive away. Vaguely she was aware that she was back on Alligator Alley, driving towards Naples. Blackness totally engulfed her. Her face was covered with tears, but she didn't feel the wetness. She couldn't feel anything except for the severe headache and the terrible anxiety. More than anything, she needed to get in control of her feelings, to be strong. For a brief moment, she thought of Terry, but that, too, disappeared into the blackness of her nightmare. She had no plan or conscious thought about what she was doing. Her movements were in the control of someone or something else.

* * *

Pilar wasn't too happy. For one thing, Deena and Christine had shown no respect toward her at all. In fact, they had all but ignored her in the restaurant. Then when they got to Shyla's house, they were more interested in rummaging through Shyla's things than spending time with her. Pilar was certain everyone had noticed it. It wasn't very nice of Shyla to just show up like that either. Why hadn't she at least called someone instead of walking in on them the way she had. She seemed upset, but if it was because Carlos' family was visiting in her home, then she would just have to get used to it. After all, family was everything. She shrugged.

KiKi was putting the two children down for a nap, and Rosa was out on the patio looking at the pool and gardens. Pilar joined her sister outside. It was a warm day; and some clouds were starting to build up in the western sky. She wiped the perspiration from her face with a tissue. She just wished that Deena and Christine had talked to her a little. She also wished that Shyla hadn't seemed so upset.

* * *

Terry finally located Wayne Carter on his cell phone at the Benvenue Country Club where he was playing a round of golf. Wayne was head of the Department of Records and Archives for the county. The two of them had become friends in college and continued to be, keeping up with each other's careers, occasionally downing a beer or two together, playing a round of golf, and helping each other out when needed. If Wayne had a legal problem, he knew he could count on Terry for advice. That was why Terry didn't mind bothering his friend on the golf course, even if it was his turn to putt on the seventeenth green, and even if it was on a Saturday.

"I take it this can't wait until Monday morning when most sane, civilized people go to work?" Wayne was eyeing a six-foot putt which, if he made it, would give him a two-stroke lead over the other three men he was playing against.

Terry took a deep breath. "It's urgent, my friend."

"OK. I'll be finished up here in another thirty minutes. Then I'll make a few phone calls. If I can't locate the people I need, I'll go in and do it myself."

"Thanks, buddy. I owe you one."

"You'll owe me more than that if I don't sink this putt."

* * *

After Terry left, Jayne took a quick shower and drove over to Ibis. She wanted to check the registration forms that Mariela had filled out when she signed up for Shyla's class. It didn't take her long to find them since Mariela was a current student.

Under the category, "Personal Background," Mariela had written in the names of three people: her father, Augusto Fanjul; her mother, Octavia Maria Santiago Fanjul, deceased; and her grandfather, Octavio Fanjul, also deceased. Nowhere was Maria Santiago Fanjul mentioned. Apparently, the grandmother was still living, though, and it was she who actually controlled the Fanjul inheritance. How odd, thought Jayne, but it still didn't shed any light on why Shyla would be named the principal beneficiary.

She put the papers back into the file and went into her office to use the telephone. Surely Shyla had gotten to West Palm Beach by now. There was no answer.

* * *

The first chapter was completed. Now all Mariela had to do was go over it and correct any glaring mistakes. She was sure she had made quite a few, because she was in such a hurry to get the story written down. After reading over it, she would run off a copy for Shyla. She could do a comprehensive edit of it later.

It was strange. Ever since returning to Trégo, all Mariela had thought about was writing this story. It were as though it was something living and tangible, needing only her presence at Trégo to be released; and it had been waiting for her to return. She had no idea of what she wanted to do when she finished writing *The Immigrant*, if anything. There were no longings pulling at her as they had in the past, and she had no other ideas for another book. Nor did she have any desire to leave Trégo.

She felt ecstatic, almost euphoric. Shyla had told her she would. There was something liberating about the process of writing, especially when writing about something she was so consumed with. *The Immigrant* was actually coming to life, and she was making it happen.

* * *

All four of them were now present: Maria, Miguel, Juan, and Jesus. Except for the colorful *ilekes* which they wore around their necks, each of the male immigrants was dressed in white representing purity of spirit; Maria, the *Iyalocha* or high priestess, dressed in black, something for which she had petitioned the *orishas* and received permission long ago.

Miguel placed the container with the chosen sacrificial animal on the mat covering the ground before the altar. Maria filled her mouth with *aguardiente*, a strong distilled liquid made from the juice of sugar cane, and sprayed it over the others as a blessing. All was quiet. As the

Iyalocha or high priestess, Maria next held up a container of *omiero,* a mixture of rain water, river water, sea water and holy water. She then combined it with the *aguardiente,* some honey, powdered eggshell, pepper, and various herbs in order to brew the mixture with fresh taro leafs.

The mixture was presented to the four cardinal points and then to the *orishas*. Maria asked them to bestow their magical powers on those who were present. She spilled a little of the *omiero* three times onto the mat, before offering the mixture to Miguel, Juan, and Jesus. All three drank. And then the three men began the chants of ancient times; the chants of Yoruba; the chants of *Regla de Ocha*.

Maria drew the required symbols on the mat using powdered eggshells mixed with earth from the roots of the cypress. The symbols were blessed and sprinkled with corn meal. A candle was lit. The *orishas* had been summoned.

Chapter Nine

Carl rushed after Shyla in an attempt to stop her from leaving, and, failing that, he would follow her back to the house. He knew that was where she would want to go. She loved her home. It was like a sanctuary to her. She felt secure there. When she drove off in spite of his protestations, he realized too late that he had left his car keys back in the office. By the time he retrieved them and ran back out to the parking lot, Shyla was gone.

He cut through the parking lot and worked his way through the small side streets, taking the shortest route back to the house. He had really screwed up this time. What in the hell was he thinking? But he could handle it. First of all, he would get rid of all those people at the house. His mother would just have to put up with the extra company for a few days. Either that, or they could go to a hotel. They weren't going to stay at Shyla's. By making them leave, it would show Shyla that he was considering her feelings, and that he understood and felt the same way. Then he would tell her how beautiful she was and how much he loved her. He would explain to her that no matter what she thought she saw at the office, it wasn't anything. She was his life and his reason for getting up each day. He had told her these things before when he was trying to convince her to marry him. It had worked. He could do it again. After all, it was true. He did love Shyla. She added something to his life that he would never get from anyone else. God he wished he hadn't screwed up.

* * *

Terry was standing in front of the living room window with the curtains opened watching the rain when the telephone rang. It was Wayne.

"I'll tell you one thing, my friend, you sure are dealing with some peculiar characters here." Wayne had searched through all the computer data files for birth certificates, death certificates, marriage licenses, green cards, immigration forms, business deals, and property deeds. "Basically, what it all boils down to is that one woman, Maria Santiago Fanjul, owns everything and has from the very beginning. Octavio is listed as her late husband, but there is no record of any marriage. But that isn't unusual since they immigrated from Cuba. They were probably married before coming to this country."

So far Wayne wasn't telling Terry anything new. "You said something about 'peculiar characters?'"

"You know how the department flags anything that might be a problem? Apparently, this Maria babe is some kind of high priestess of some ancient off-shoot of the Santeria religion. Something called *Regla de Ocha*. Its origins date back to the slave trade when Yoruba natives were forcibly transported from Africa to the Caribbean, sometime during the sixteenth century. During the communist revolution, Santeria fell out of favor and was actively suppressed in Cuba. *Regla de Ocha* was completely eliminated because of the powerful position it gave to women. That was probably why Maria and the others came to Florida. Now, here is where it gets sticky. The religious practices and beliefs are passed down orally from the high priestess or chief *orisha* to a female blood relative who is supposedly blessed by all the other *orishas* or gods. *Orisha* literally means "head guardian." That is the only way it can survive, so you can imagine how important it is that there be someone in the family to carry on this tradition. Going on what I am able to find out, Maria must be about seventy-eight years old now. I would think that finding a replacement for her, a young female blood relative, is top priority. Oh, and Terry, a couple of other things. They believe in stuff like soul transferences and soul unions; and they also believe in animal sacrifices. Does any of this information help you?"

"I don't know yet," said Terry. "I'll tell you later. By the way, how did you do on that putt?"

"I sunk it."

After Wayne hung up, Terry went over his notes. He had on numerous occasions gone to Trégo, usually having to do with some legal matter. A few times he had been invited to stay for supper with Augusto Fanjul and Mariela. He had been amazed that there were so few servants who actually took care of Trégo. Each time he had gone, there had always been the same servants. Thinking back on it, all of the servants had been men except for one woman, and Mariela had called her RaRa. An unusual name for a Cuban. Unless it was a nickname that Mariela had given to her as a child. In fact, there was a good possibility that RaRa was some sort of nickname for Maria and Mariela didn't even know that she was her grandmother, which would explain why she hadn't included her name on the registration papers Jayne had mentioned. If RaRa was the high priestess or *Iyalocha,* it was probably something that had been kept secret from Mariela for her own protection, a belief carried over from the days in Cuba since she stood in line to inherit the position.

He was familiar with the 1993 US Supreme Court ruling made in favor of Santerians, allowing the use of animal sacrifices based on religious grounds. From what he understood of Santeria, "the way of the saints," elements of Catholicism had been introduced into the ancient religion, and many of the African gods were now identified by the names of Catholic saints. There was nothing about the basic "tenets" of the faith that encouraged harm to humans. If anything, its purpose was to offer hope and solution through ancestor reverence and nature worship. The one piece that he still didn't have an answer to, however, was why Shyla was named principal beneficiary in Maria's will instead of Mariela. It just didn't make sense, especially if it was all tied in to the religion. Shyla certainly wasn't a blood relative. Unless there was some connection to their belief in soul union.

He picked up the phone and dialed Jayne's number. He wanted to find out if she had been able to reach Shyla yet.

* * *

The rain was coming down harder now. At some point, Shyla had turned on the windshield wipers and the headlights. It was already starting to get dark, and the thick rain clouds made it even more so. The glare on the wet road from approaching cars made it difficult to see.

Another kind of darkness surrounded Shyla; she felt only numbness. Occasionally a thought would float to the surface, break through and reveal itself, and then disappear back into the dark hole. One of those thoughts was that Shyla's marriage had been a total sham from the very beginning. Carl had wanted to marry her, but it wasn't because he loved her. There had to have been other reasons, reasons which she didn't understand. It also occurred to her that she had changed everything in her life in order to accommodate Carl and his mother. After all, he had sacrificed for her by giving up his daughters when they wouldn't accept her, or so she thought. He didn't want to have that conflict in their marriage, he had told her, because he loved her so much. But, of course, that was a lie as well. His relationship with his daughters had continued, secretly. Otherwise, why would they have been at her house, going through her things, unless Carl had invited them there along with the rest of his family. Only Shyla had been left out. Once again.

She remembered an incident that had occurred shortly after they were married. Carl had brought home a computer disc, one of those golf games that you played on the computer. He told Shyla one of the consultants from work had given it to him. Later she discovered a receipt where Carl had charged it to his credit card. When she asked him about it, he insisted that the consultant had given it to him, until she showed him the receipt.

What had disturbed her the most about it wasn't that he had spent the money, but that he felt he had to lie to her. If he lied about the small things, she could only imagine what big things he was hiding. He told her that was the only time he had lied to her, and it was because he felt embarrassed about spending money on such a silly thing, especially knowing he wasn't contributing that much toward paying their bills. She understood and had quickly forgotten about it—until now.

* * *

Jayne was concerned to the point that she had George on the ready to contact his friend with the Florida Highway Patrol. She had tried calling Shyla's house several times, and each time someone speaking Spanish had answered the phone and then hung up. Shyla should have already been there hours ago. She would try one more time, and if she didn't get her, she would get George to notify the highway patrol. This time a man answered.

"Hello, this is Jayne Sinclare. Is Shyla there?"

Carl recognized the name. It was Shyla's friend at the Ibis Institute. "Jayne, this is Carl, Shyla's husband." He paused briefly. "Listen, there has been sort of a misunderstanding here, and I don't know where Shyla is."

Jayne took a deep breath. "Can you tell me what has happened? Maybe I can help."

Carl wouldn't go into detail. Only that several members of his family were visiting from Argentina, and something had occurred at his office which Shyla completely misunderstood. Jayne could imagine. The Latin lover didn't know Shyla was coming home for the weekend and had probably been showing his ass—in more ways than one. And judging from all the racket she had heard on the telephone, his mother and all the rest of his relatives had moved into Shyla's house while she was away.

"If you see her, would you please tell her to call me. It's urgent, Carl."

He said he would, but that didn't exactly reassure Jayne. After hanging up she called Terry to tell him what she had found out. Then she got George to call his friend.

* * *

Mariela sang a song from her childhood as she dressed to go into Naples. It was something she used to sing to her imaginary friend, Eleggua, when she had played in the clearing among the cypress trees, like the forest-roaming wild child in John Milton's poem, *L'Allegro*. RaRa had taught it to her. Why she was thinking of it now, she had no idea. RaRa had taught her a lot of things, incidental things like certain butterflies and moths exude the same scent as the flower they visit. Or, leaves three, leave be. And about the magic that came from the beautiful cowrie shells. Simple things, really.

She had washed her hair and showered, and slipped on a pair of blue jeans and a long-sleeved shirt. It was raining so it might be a little cool out. She put the copy of her first chapter into a brown envelope, wrote Shyla's name on it, and, grabbing an umbrella in the stand next to the front door, made a dash for the garage. It was starting to get late, but Shyla hadn't said anything about going anywhere so it didn't occur to Mariela to call first. Besides, if Shyla wasn't in, she would just leave the envelope with her manuscript in it at Shyla's cottage. Shyla would find it when she got back.

The wind buffeted the small car and the rain seemed to come in waves, making it difficult for Mariela to keep the small car on her side of the road. She felt so happy about her progress. She wouldn't stay while Shyla read her first chapter. She just wanted to give it to Shyla. That way Shyla could read it when she felt like it.

* * *

The drumming was loud and pronounced, its rhythm distinctive now. The chanting continued. Maria began to shake and shudder with convulsions, causing her to fall to the mat. She lay still for several moments. She had gone to another place and, her followers believed, to another time. Juan, and Jesus rubbed cocoa butter onto her hands and feet while Miguel blew into her ears and mouth to restore the calm. The drum beat became louder. Minutes passed, and Maria, now restored, stood and began to dance to a specific rhythm while chanting. Miguel removed the sacrificial animal from its small cage. Maria took the chicken into her hands and held it up to the images of Christ and Saint Barbara and to the three men who were present. Deftly, she ripped off the chicken's head and sprinkled its blood on Miguel, Juan, and Jesus. It was the blessing of the *orisha*. *Ébo* was now complete.

* * *

The thunder rumbled a little louder and the wind picked up out of the west as the rain continued hammering the roof of Shyla's car. She was reminded of the night her first husband died while she stood by helplessly watching the paramedics as they futilely attempted to resuscitate him, and how only a few weeks later Hurricane Andrew slammed into the southeast coast of Florida. Her parents were living in Homestead at the time, but had come up to stay with her since she was alone and all the forecasts were predicting the storm to make landfall at West Palm Beach. It was two days later that they learned about the "wobble" in the storm's path, ironically sparing West Palm Beach but causing a direct hit on Homestead. She and her parents drove south, dodging felled trees, live electrical wires, and tons of trash and debris littering the highway until they eventually reached the pile of rubble that had once been her parents' home. Even the bark had been stripped from what remained of the trees. The sun was so bright that day, it seemed garish and mocking, shining on so much devastation. Everything was eerily quiet and still. There was no sign of life anywhere other than a dog who was rolling in the dirt nearby yelping either from injury or from the shock of having everything familiar and loved snatched away by something it didn't understand. This memory, too, like the others, slowly disappeared into the darkness.

For a moment, she stepped outside of herself, observing and mentally recording. Even as a child she had been the one to remain on the outside of whatever was happening so she could watch the interaction of people and events take place. Many times she wondered if that childish curiosity, and her ability to remove herself from any situation in order to objectively observe and scrutinize it, is what had determined that she be a writer. Or had she been born a writer, and that was the reason for her passion to observe life separate and apart. That was the place where she was now. Separate and apart. She watched her hands gripping the steering wheel, she felt the warmth of the tears on her face, she observed the blinking lights of on-coming traffic. And she felt an unbearable, crippling pain, like that yelping dog after the storm.

Shyla reached the city limits of Naples, but she didn't notice. Neither did she notice the pick-up truck skidding through the intersection as she approached it, just before it slammed into the small red sports car. She had fallen back into the dark hole where she couldn't feel or think. Only when the airbag exploded into her breasts, crushing her chest and ribs, did she realize she had been involved in an accident.

Chapter Ten

Carl helped the taxi driver load all the luggage into the cab. He wanted to be sure he was at the house when Shyla returned. With his mother refusing to drive with so many people in her car, he had called a taxi to take his cousin and her two kids to his mother's house. His mother, with Aunt Rosa in the seat next to her, sat with lips tight and arms folded, in her own car on the street where Carl had parked it moments earlier. Nothing had worked out to her satisfaction, and now she felt she was literally being shoved out the door. He would probably have hell to pay for it later, but right now he had to do whatever he thought Shyla would want.

After they were gone, he went back into the house and started cleaning up. He closed the doors going out onto the patio that had been left open, as well as the door going from the house to the garage, and picked up the sofa cushions that were on the floor. Everything was in a mess. For a fleeting instant he thought about trying to locate that woman who had started doing some cleaning for Shyla. Then he saw the little china clock that had belonged to Shyla's great grandmother, the one thing that had survived the hurricane that destroyed her parents' home a few years back. It was on the floor, shattered. He thought he was going to vomit. He found a plastic bag and picked up all the pieces. He would put it away, out of sight for now and tell Shyla about it later.

Then he went into the master bedroom. Most of the drawers were open. Shyla's lingerie was thrown on the bed, her jewelry scattered on the dresser. He folded the garments the best he could and put them away. A couple of her gold chains had knots in them. He would try to fix them later. The rest of the stuff he placed back in her jewelry box.

Shyla's Initiative

For the first time since marrying Shyla, he felt scared. If he lost her, he didn't know what he would do. For one thing, he wouldn't be able to afford a place of his own, not unless he went back to court to get the divorce settlement changed. That would take a lawyer, and even more money. The only other option would be to move in with his mother, something he refused to even think about. Somehow he would have to convince Shyla that they belonged together. He had made some mistakes, but it wouldn't happen again. He would make it up to her.

Right now he needed to do something to keep from worrying. He went into the kitchen and pulled out a bag of flour. He would fix Shyla some home-made spaghetti. She liked that. He would make it just for her. He set up his cuisinart for making the pasta dough and got out the large skillet for the sauce. He would even set the table with candles to make it romantic.

* * *

Jayne got the news first, thanks to George's friend. She immediately called Terry and told him what had happened. There had been a terrible accident, the rain-slick roads, a sports car had been hit by a truck and totaled, one person was killed, someone else suffered a fractured leg and facial cuts. Shyla was badly shaken and bruised, her car also totaled. The ambulance had taken her to the County Memorial Hospital for observation. Then she called Carl and told him basically the same thing which, upon reflection, seemed strange that she would have called Terry before Shyla's husband.

George insisted on driving since Jayne was so upset. They arrived at the hospital moments before Terry. George offered to wait in the lounge area while Terry and Jayne quickly located the room and went in. Shyla appeared to be sleeping.

"Where have you been?" asked Shyla looking at the two of them.

Jayne rushed up to the bed and took her friend's hand. "My god, Shyla, we have been so worried about you."

Shyla glanced over at Terry and smiled. "Hello."

"Hello. How do you feel?" he asked moving closer.

"My boobs hurt."

Jayne and Terry looked at each other, not sure they understood what she had said.

"You see, when the airbag deployed, it just about crushed what little bit I have."

Jayne nodded. She had never heard Shyla talk like this before. It was probably due to some medication they had given her for the pain.

"Is there anything you need that I can get for you?" Terry wanted so badly to touch Shyla to prove to himself that she was all right. He placed his hand on top of Jayne's hand which was still holding onto Shyla.

"I would love to have a cup of good Cuban coffee. Do you think they have any around here?"

Jayne caught her breath. Shyla didn't even like coffee. She always drank tea. "Let me see if I can find some," she said blinking at Terry with one eyebrow arched.

"Thanks, girlfriend. That will give me a chance to talk to Terry."

When she left the room, Shyla explained what had happened, at least all that had happened leading up to the accident. She didn't remember too much about driving back to Naples from West Palm Beach, and she didn't remember anything about the accident itself. She did remember, in vivid detail, however, everything that had taken place before. Finding all of Carl's relatives at her house, the noise and confusion, and then finding Carl with his "office mate," as he called her. Now Shyla needed Terry's help.

"How fast can I get a divorce?"

Terry pulled up a chair and sat next to the bed. "In Florida there is something called a 'Quick Dissolution of Marriage,' which is the most expedient way to get a divorce, providing that both parties agree to the divorce, there are no custodial issues involving children, and the settlement of all personal property matters can be worked out in advance."

"Can you help me with it, or do I need to find someone in West Palm Beach?"

"I'll start on it tonight after I leave here. Don't worry about a thing. I'll take care it. I will need to get some information from you, but once I get all the paper work completed, it will just be a matter of the two of you standing in front of a judge and signing them."

Just then Carl came rushing into the room. "Shyla, I got here as soon as I could. Are you all right?" He rushed past Terry who got up from the chair and moved out of the way. "What a terrible thing to happen. You won't have to do anything. Just rest. I am here now to take care of you." He immediately began plumping her pillow.

Terry left the room, closing the door behind him in order to give them privacy. He didn't need to be there. Jayne came back shortly with a large Styrofoam cup of hot black Cuban coffee. Heaven only knew where she had been able to locate it. She went into the room just long enough to give it to Shyla.

"Did she say anything?" asked Terry when Jayne came back out.

"She told Carl she wanted him and his mother's fat ass out of her life." Jayne looked at him wide-eyed. "Terry, I have never heard Shyla talk like that; words like 'boobs' and 'ass' just aren't in her vocabulary. She had Carl in tears."

"It's probably just the shock of everything. She might have even sustained a concussion. I wouldn't worry about it too much."

Jayne tried unsuccessfully to suppress a nervous giggle. "Actually, I think it's kind of a good thing. Shyla has always been so passive and easily taken advantage of." She then told Terry that while going past the nurses' station after getting the coffee, she had found out who the other victim was in the accident—the one who had been killed. It was Mariela Fanjul.

Terry ran his hand through his hair. "Oh, god. Her father will be crushed." He shook his head in disbelief and looked down, letting his legal mind spring into action. As legal counsel to the Fanjul family, he would have a lot to do. "I need to go take care of some things," he told Jayne. "Do you want me to help you locate George?"

"No, thanks anyway. I'm sure he'll just wait for me in the lobby. I want to hang around here for a while so I can talk to Shyla a little more after Carl leaves. I have a feeling he won't be staying very long." The situation was almost laughable had it not been for the fact that Mariela was now dead.

Terry nodded. "Tell Shyla I will see her tomorrow. Tell Shyla . . ."

Jayne smiled. She knew more than Terry was even able to admit to himself. He had been so happy and upbeat since meeting Shyla. It was obvious he had strong feelings for her. "I'll tell her you are wishing her a speedy recovery and that you will see her soon."

"Yes. Tell her that," said Terry.

***

Carl was so busy fussing over Shyla, plumping pillows, straightening sheets, pouring water into the glass on her bedside table, that he didn't even notice Terry when he first got to Shyla's room. He probably didn't notice him when he left either. This was his chance to really show Shyla how much he loved her, and that he would do anything to make up for the fool he had been.

"Are you in much pain, my love? Are you comfortable?" He sat down in the chair Terry had been sitting in moments earlier and clutched at Shyla's hand. He smiled. "You look so beautiful, I don't know how you do it." It bothered him a little that Shyla still hadn't said anything to him. She just stared at him with a slight smile on her lips. He adjusted the way he was sitting in the chair. "Mother sends her love. She wanted to come with me to see you, she is so worried about you, but I thought the drive would be too much for her, and her sister is visiting her for a few weeks."

Shyla stirred and pulled her hand free. "Carl, I want you to listen to me carefully because I don't want to repeat myself. If you don't understand anything that I tell you, then ask me to explain it. All right?"

"Of course, my love. Anything." He leaned forward so he could be closer to Shyla. He didn't want her to have to strain her voice.

"I have put up with your lies and deceit for eight months now. I have catered to you, your mother, and all your relatives since the day after we got married. I have heard nothing but complaints and criticism from your mother, which you have condoned through your silence, even though I have done everything humanly possible to make her life and yours easier. You have done nothing to support me or my wants other than fix me breakfast every morning, which I hate. Neither have you done anything toward making our marriage work. On the contrary, you have gone out of your way to establish a secret life with your daughters, your mother, your relatives, and your so-called office-mate. So this is the way it is going to be. You will return to West Palm Beach now and remove everything and everyone that does not belong in my house or to me personally, and that includes your mother's fat ass. I do not want you to spend another night in my house. I do not want to see or hear from you until the day we go before the judge to sign the divorce papers. Is there anything about what I am saying that you don't understand?"

Carl hadn't moved. He heard everything Shyla said, but couldn't believe it was Shyla saying it. She was so calm about it. She didn't even look the same. He could feel tears welling up once more in his eyes and start running down his cheeks. It didn't do any good. Shyla told him to get out. When he didn't move, she repeated it, only this time she said it in Spanish.

* * *

Rosa fixed a cup of hot *maté* tea for Pilar and served it to her in bed. As soon as Carl called to tell her of Shyla's accident, she had one of her spells. She wanted to go with Carl to the hospital where they had taken Shyla in Naples, but Carl had insisted that he go alone. It would have taken him an extra thirty minutes to go pick up his mother. As it was, he could make it in an hour and a half if he really hurried.

"What have I done to deserve this," Pilar cried. "There has been so much tragedy in my life. First Carlos abandoning me for that awful woman, Ana. Then his father passing on. My own grandchildren ignore me. And now this. I just don't think I can cope with any more."

"Now, now," Rosa clicked her tongue. She wanted to be comforting to her younger sister, but she honestly couldn't see why Pilar was so upset. It was Shyla who had been hurt in the accident, not Pilar. Besides, from the stories she had gotten, Pilar didn't even especially like Shyla. "Carlos said he would call you from the hospital. Everything will be all right." Rosa disappeared into Pilar's large walk-in closet and began to unpack her things.

Pilar sipped her tea and lay back on the bed pillows that Rosa had fluffed for her to ease the stiffness in her back. She wondered how long Shyla would have to stay in the hospital. And what was she doing back in Naples anyway? Pilar knew Shyla was upset when she found all of them in her house earlier that day, but was that enough to make her want to drive all the way back to Naples? Now Carlos would probably want to stay with her instead of being here where she needed him to help her entertain her family.

KiKi and her two children had finally gone to bed in the spare room. She could hear Rosa in her closet, scraping hangers across the rod, dropping things, and moving things around. She sighed and shrugged. Maybe if Shyla was going to stay in the hospital for a few days, they could still go to her house. She would suggest it when Carlos called.

* * *

Terry had been brought up in Little River, a small, lazy, backwater town that straddled the border between North and South Carolina. What there was of it sprawled along the banks of a brackish body of water the locals called a river, but, in actuality, was an extension of a larger body of water, the Little River Sound, which eventually spilled into the Atlantic Ocean. It was a fishing village, primarily, with a few outsiders living in the area, like the Sawyer's, who had other interests.

The Sawyer home was a large, two-story edifice, with dark green shutters framing each of the many windows. It displayed neither beauty nor grace. The bulk of it was painted white for the most part, although positioned in such close proximity to the salt air and damp sea breezes, it was next to impossible to keep anything coated with paint for very long. The house perched on a slight rise in a field of green, peppered with gnarled, moss-covered live oaks and overlooking the river. There was nothing fancy or architecturally pleasing about it, but it was comfortable for Terry, his younger brother, Tom, their parents, and the woman who worked as a live-in housekeeper and surrogate parent whenever Mr. and Mrs. Sawyer had to leave the boys in order to go on one of their numerous work-related trips.

As the oldest, and also being an over-achiever, a trait more common than not among first-borns, Terry left home his first summer out of high school in order to continue his formal education in Florida. Initially, he thought he wanted to continue the work his parents had been involved in for so many years and declared his major in paranormal psychology. It was later, however, that he discovered another interest, and even though it delayed his getting a degree, he went into law.

Tom, Terry's brother, remained close to home. He married shortly after high school graduation, became a real estate agent, and had three children in quick succession. When Terry's father died, and then his mother six months later, it seemed perfectly logical that Tom and his young growing family move into the old Sawyer homestead. It would certainly give them the room they desperately needed compared to the small three bedroom, one bathroom house they were in. And it was an ideal location to bring up their children. Terry, for his part, took all of the many books and boxes of files and research materials that had been accumulated by his parents over the years and stored in various closets throughout the old house. Tom had no interest in any of it, and by this time, his wife welcomed any storage space they could get.

Terry had loaded all the boxes, with the help of his brother, into the small van he had leased for that purpose and hauled everything back to his newly renovated office in Naples. One by one he carried each box up the stairs to a large closet where they remained untouched, until now.

Shyla's Initiative

It was the timing of everything. First those wills, the last of which named Shyla primary beneficiary to the Fanjul fortune. Then the death of Mariela. Shyla's change in behavior could easily be justified by the trauma she experienced from the accident, or was it caused by something else? His parents had taught him that it was the timing that mattered most in events out of the ordinary.

The information his friend, Wayne, had gotten for him triggered something in the back of Terry's mind. Something his parents had shown him when he was still planning to study parapsychology. He would start preparing Shyla's divorce papers, but first he needed to find something. Back at his office in an upstairs hall closet he pulled out several cardboard boxes. In them were textbooks and reams of notes, all carefully indexed and labeled. Finally, after dumping everything out, he found what he was looking for. It was a small paperback written in 1970 by noted psychiatrist Dr. Lynden Boyd. The title of the book was simply *Walk-ins*. His parents had shown it to him because they knew of Terry's interest in their own research on the subject of soul union at the time. Terry remembered he had even highlighted certain passages. He came across one of them which he was looking for:

> *The primary issue in the lives of many who undergo soul transference or soul union is divorce. Sometimes it is the breakup of a marriage that prompts the Walk-out to withdraw. The feeling of disappointment and betrayal, or perhaps failure, is too great to live with. Other times it results from the inability of a spouse to live with an entity different from the original occupant of the body.*

He read more:

A Walk-in inherits the memory patterns of the Walk-out, but just as we can no longer remember many happenings of our earlier years, so a Walk-in would have even greater difficulty in bringing to mind things of an unimportant nature that had not involved his or her own emotional system.

He put everything back in the box to carry downstairs. This would have to be researched further, but he felt he was on to something. It might explain Shyla's new fondness for Cuban coffee and the change in her personality. Mariela was the only living blood relative directly descended from her grandmother, and, therefore, would have been the natural heir apparent to the *Iyalocha* or head guardian position. If, however, something had been wrong with Mariela that would have prevented her from inheriting the position, and Maria knew it, then the next logical step would be to find someone close to Mariela in which a soul union could take place since there was no other female blood relative. Someone like Shyla. In fact, Mariela's soul would become part of Shyla's, sharing Shyla's body, her character, and her personality. Things started by Mariela that had been important to her would now be important to Shyla, and she would feel responsible for completing whatever they were. Like writing. Shyla had told him Mariela wanted to expand her short story into a novel. If there had been a soul union, now Shyla would feel the responsibility to complete it.

Once, Terry's parents had taken him on one of their "haunts" to an area located just outside of Lumberton, North Carolina. It was there only a few years earlier that a small group of people had been discovered living in a settlement of several wooden shacks and lean-tos that peppered a dirt crossroads some distance off one side of the main highway. The strange thing about it was no one could understand the language of the people living there. Scientists came from everywhere to study these people and determine their origin. There was speculation that the inhabitants were some distant, surviving remnant of a heretofore unknown Indian tribe. The community seemed to be tribal in nature, and it had a leader, even though nothing else seemed to match that theory. It was even discussed that legislation be introduced that would proclaim the small band of people indigenous and, therefore, entitled to certain rights from the United States government. But nothing ever came of it. Eventually, these people simply became known as the "high yellows," due primarily to the color of their skin, and were for the most part left alone and forgotten.

What had created a renewed interest in the "high yellows" and had led the Sawyers to the settlement was a report that a soul union had taken place between one of the young males and the elderly tribe leader at the time of his death. Most experts dismissed the claim, stating simply there was too little to go on. The tribe leader was old and childless, and creating this story at the time of his death was his way of selecting the next leader as well as creating a sort of dynasty. Some even suggested that it was an attempt to bring in tourism to the otherwise economically-deprived area. Terry's parents felt otherwise, however. After spending weeks collecting data and observing the young Indian boy and the other tribe members, it was their conclusion that a soul union had indeed taken place. Terry was nine years old at the time, as was the Indian boy. Thinking about it now, he still could remember feeling that he was in the presence of an old man whenever he was with the young boy.

Terry sat down on the steps. It was all too overwhelming and absurd. Yet, he had studied enough cases involving this and related subjects to know that it was possible. It certainly wasn't beyond belief.

***

Maria lay unconscious on the mat in front of the altar. The drum was silent, the sacrificed animal had been removed. It would be prepared and cooked later. Order had been restored, the sacrificial area cleansed. Only a single lit candle remained to remind the four remaining immigrants what had taken place. She slowly regained consciousness, and once she was fully recovered, Miguel helped her to stand. She would remember nothing of the events that took place.

Quietly she returned to the west wing. She would make it ready for the newcomer's arrival. Maria did not weep, for there was no reason for sadness. She had done the only thing she could to save Mariela. Now *Regla de Ocha* would also be saved, this time in written form, and passed down to the next generations. They all had been blessed; the *orishas* had provided the answer.

***

The rain had stopped and the sky was clear. The moon was full and startlingly bright. Carl couldn't stop thinking, planning, figuring out what his next move would be. Shyla had told him she didn't want him spending another night in her house, and for him to drive back, get his stuff out, and never come back. He had never seen her so angry. She had used words that even he never used before, some of them in Spanish. Christ, when did she learn to speak Spanish? In the end, all he could do was agree to do as she said and return to West Palm Beach. He had already stopped twice alongside the road because of diarrhea. He always had trouble with his bowels when he got tense, and he was definitely tense. The best thing for him to do right now was to do what Shyla wanted. He would return to the house, get his things, and go stay with his mother for a day or so until Shyla got back. Then he would talk to her. By then she wouldn't be so angry. He would send her flowers, she loved flowers, and sentimental cards, she liked those too. He would make some on his computer to give them a personal touch. He would get her to come around. Right now it was just the shock of the accident and all.

Carl put on his right turn signal and pulled off to the side of the road. His bowels were acting up again.

* * *

It was shortly after midnight, and Pilar still hadn't heard anything from Carl. Rosa was asleep next to her in her queen-size bed; it had been a long day. After fixing another cup of *maté*, Pilar heard a car in the driveway. She went to the front window and peered out. Carl was unloading what looked like clothes on hangers and a cardboard box. She rushed to open the door for him. "I'll have to sleep on the couch," was all he said. He struggled to set the box on the floor and then carried his clothes into Pilar's bedroom closet. She followed him, trying to be quiet so she wouldn't wake her sister. Carl shoved some hangers to one side of the rod to make room for his things.

Back out in the living room he started to undress. "Shyla has some bruising, and she will be sore for a few days, but other than that she will be fine."

"Why are you staying here?" Pilar asked.

Carl simply couldn't deal with anything else. He had just driven over two hundred miles in a little more than three hours. His gut felt like it had a knife blade sticking through it, and, frankly, at that moment, he didn't care if he lived or died. "I'll tell you about it some other time. Right now I just want to get some sleep.

Pilar scuffled over to the hall closet where she kept an extra pillow and blanket and got them out for her son. Then she scuffled back to bed. She would wait until tomorrow, but then she expected to get some answers. She would also ask him about staying at Shyla's house.

Chapter Eleven

Shyla spent the one night at the hospital and then returned to Hemingway Cottage. Other than some slight soreness around her ribs and chest area, Shyla felt remarkably well. Her energy was up, her attitude was good, and she hadn't experienced any anxiety or headaches since the night of the accident. She thought that perhaps the shock of everything still hadn't worn off and eventually the rage would come. It didn't.

Jayne, on the other hand, was having fits. "You need to rest. You have been through a terrible ordeal. Come to my house and stay, at least until you get over the shock of everything. I don't want you teaching the class next week." But Shyla, with her new initiative, insisted on having her way; that being, she would stay at Hemingway Cottage for the remainder of the week and finish teaching the course in creative writing just as she had originally planned. Then she would return to West Palm Beach and deal with whatever she had to there. She explained to Jayne, "Besides, I still have four more assignments to give, including my favorite which is writing a one-page character sketch of the person whom you least like." She flipped a lock of hair from her neck, something which for some reason reminded Jayne of Mariela. "My students expect it, and I want to keep my sterling reputation."

Shyla also wanted to in some way express her sympathy to Mariela's father. When she asked Terry about it, he told her that he had found out there would be a private service at Trégo, just for the immediate family and personal servants. No one else would be attending. Naturally, Mariela would be buried on the estate, next to her mother in the family cemetery.

Oddly enough, on the day the private service was to take place, Shyla received a dozen red roses. The enclosed card had only two names printed on it: Augusto Fanjul and Maria Santiago Fanjul. Included with the card was a cowrie shell. That night she wrote a long letter to Mr. Fanjul to thank him and Ms. Maria Fanjul for the thoughtful gesture, but also to tell him of her fondness for his daughter and how happy she was to have gotten to know her. "She had a gift that so few have," Shyla wrote; "the ability to write her thoughts and feelings in a way that touched everyone. I regret I wasn't able to know her longer. I will deeply miss her."

Three days later, a highway patrolman who had been on duty the evening of the accident brought Shyla a brown envelope with her name written on it. It had been found in the red sports car. He thought she might want to have it. After he left, Shyla opened it. It was Mariela's first chapter of *The Immigrant.*

Shyla knew what it would say even before she read it. It was beautifully written. Shyla also knew what the next chapter would be and the next and the one after that. She knew the story of *The Immigrant* as though she had experienced the hardships on that initial voyage from Cuba herself. She also understood the role of The Guardian, the sacred *orisha,* and she respected it as though she were the one who would one day inherit that role.

She tucked the manuscript safely away with the cowrie shell and some other personal items. As soon as her course at Ibis was completed, there were a number of things she needed to take care of, beginning with getting her divorce. She also needed to decide on another car, once the insurance company acted on her claim. Until then, she would lease something. She dreaded going home; she couldn't stop thinking about that last time she was there and the people and the mess she found, before she found Carl. She would have to go back, of course, and face whatever was there. She didn't doubt that Carl had done exactly what she had told him to do, so she didn't have to worry about him bothering her. It was everything else that worried her—like her great grandmother's broken clock. Once she dealt with these things, and she would, her mind would be free and clear. Then she would start writing *The Immigrant*.

* * *

Jayne couldn't get over the change in Shyla ever since the accident. She tried to explain it to Terry and wound up saying that Shyla had been like a beautiful but unseasoned filet mignon that was now seasoned to perfection. It was during lunch that she said it, she was hungry, which explains the reference to food, and the two of them were waiting for Shyla to join them. "Do you know that before all of this happened, Carl would serve her breakfast in bed every morning?"

"Well, I guess the guy can't be all bad," Terry responded sarcastically.

"I think he was just trying to control her. The point is, Shyla has always hated breakfast, but she forced it down anyway so she wouldn't hurt Carl's feelings. She always put other people's feelings before her own. I bet she wouldn't do that now. She is still Shyla, but more so."

The biggest change in Shyla that Jayne had noticed was her self-confidence, which Jayne found amazing considering what Shyla had told her about the events leading up to the accident. Shyla was more assertive, and she laughed more. Before, she had always been so serious. She even carried herself differently when she walked, not to mention her new-found taste for Cuban coffee. Of course, these were things that only someone who knew Shyla well would notice. Jayne certainly noticed, and so did Terry.

"She acts like she feels great, it's just that I keep noticing little things about her that weren't there before the accident. Nothing bad. Just different. What do you think?" Jayne asked Terry for the third time. "Do you think she is all right?"

"I think she is terrific. Maybe she was just feeling the anxiety of an unhappy marriage before, and now that she has decided to get a divorce, she feels a certain relief. That happens." He didn't want to get into the soul union thing with Jayne; not yet, anyway. He really didn't have that much to go on, and even if he did, there was nothing he could do about it, especially if it was somehow tied in to the Fanjul's belief in Santeria.

Jayne didn't get a chance to respond because at that moment Shyla came rushing up to the table. She couldn't wait to tell them about a manuscript that had been turned in by one of the students. It was the one-page character sketch assignment written about someone the writer disliked. This particular writer had chosen to write about the "cucumber" character. "Don't you just love it?" Shyla sat down at the table laughing.

* * *

Over the next few days Terry spent his time driving back and forth between Ibis, Trégo and his office. He saw Shyla every day, getting information from her that was needed in order to complete the divorce papers. Things like the prenuptial agreement between her and Carl and their financial statements were back in West Palm Beach. He could get those things from her after she returned home. In the meantime, he would get everything else completed and a court date set.

Actually, he could have easily gotten all he needed from Shyla in one meeting, except that he also wanted to see her to make sure she was doing all right, which she seemed to be. He usually tried to time it where they could have lunch or dinner together as well. A couple of times Jayne joined them, but the other days Terry took her to new places off campus. Shyla seemed to have no regrets or remorse over her marriage with Carl or the divorce. She talked about Carl freely and without bitterness. She just wanted to get everything taken care of as quickly as possible.

There were a number of things that needed to be tended to at Trégo also, as a result of Mariela's death. Her own will, for one thing, the disposal of her personal property, insurance, and various other matters that Terry either took care of personally or at least advised Augusto on how to best handle whatever it was. At the end of each of these visits, strangely enough, Augusto always asked about Shyla.

Then Miguel showed up at Terry's office. It was Friday and Terry was returning to his office from having lunch with Shyla. Even though it was during business hours and Terry's secretary was in, Miguel waited on the front porch as before.

"Hello, Miguel," said Terry climbing out of his car. He walked up on the porch. "Would you like to come in?"

Miguel shook his head and handed Terry a small white envelope. Terry opened it and read: *Mr. Augusto Fanjul and Maria Santiago Fanjul at home tomorrow evening for dinner at eight o'clock.*

Terry had to read it a couple of times before he realized that it was an invitation asking him to join Augusto Fanjul and Maria for dinner the following evening. Miguel was waiting for his answer.

"Tell them I will be delighted to join them for dinner tomorrow evening."

Miguel nodded and left.

How quaint, thought Terry, although strange might have been a better word. As many times as he had been to Trégo, this was the first time he had been formally invited for dinner. Also for the first time he would finally get to meet Maria Santiago Fanjul, the person whose name appeared on the wills as sole owner of the Fanjul fortune. Again his instincts were alerted. He immediately thought of Shyla. At least the envelope Miguel had given him didn't contain another will from The Guardian, but this invitation was like a summons. Shyla would be gone by then. She had already told him she would be returning to West Palm Beach on Saturday morning. He would contact her there, at her home, once he got the court date set and if anything new came up. They had set a time for him to call in the evenings, in case she wasn't answering her phone. In the meantime, she would gather the remaining information he needed to complete the divorce documents.

* * *

It took longer for Shyla to tell Jayne goodbye than it did to make the drive from Naples to West Palm Beach. Jayne finally agreed to let Shyla go only if she promised to call her the second she got home, she promised to call if she needed anything, and she promised that they would plan a girls' outing the first week of October. Ibis was closed for fall break then, and Jayne would have some time off.

When Shyla pulled into her driveway a couple of hours later, it wasn't as traumatic as she thought it would be. Since Carl wasn't there, the two-car garage was empty. Shyla parked in the middle. She unlocked the back door, walked into her house, and called Jayne. Then she disconnected the telephone, and for the next thirty minutes she just wandered from room to room, opening a cabinet here, a drawer there. That was how she discovered the plastic bag that held all the broken pieces of her great grandmother's clock. She took the bag out to the garage and put it in the trash barrel.

Carl had obviously cleaned up everything before he left. Or maybe Evelyn had been in to clean. She still hadn't paid her. The house looked nice. It smelled fresh. But there was something different. The strong emotional attachment Shyla had felt for her house was no longer present. It could have been anyone's pretty house. Over twelve years of her life had been spent in that house, eight of her novels had been written there, not to mention all of the articles, short stories, and poems she had produced. She felt nothing. Everything was at once familiar and yet unfamiliar.

After she unpacked she changed the sheets and threw in a load of wash. Then she went to the grocery store to pick up some milk and cereal and a few other things she would need. Feeling that everything was back in place, she started going through the mail. The check from the automobile insurance company was there. She could go ahead and get a car now. That would be one less thing to worry with. There was also a note from Terry telling her that he hoped she found everything all right on her return to West Palm Beach. He had thoughtfully mailed it the day before.

* * *

Carl had been trying to call Shyla repeatedly on the telephone but with no success. Finally on Saturday he started getting a recorded message from the phone company saying there was a problem with the line, which probably meant she was home but had disconnected the phone. She did that occasionally when she was trying to write.

He only told Pilar that Shyla was unhappy with finding everyone at her house like that. She wasn't prepared for it. As soon as she rested some though, they would be able to patch things up, he was sure. Pilar had shrugged and muttered something about "nothing lost" which produced an instant flare of anger in Carl. As always, he managed to keep it under control. Getting into an argument with his mother would only make things worse, especially now.

In the meantime, because Carl was now staying at Pilar's house, KiKi and her two kids decided to go to Orlando earlier than they had originally planned, thus relieving the crowded conditions. Maybe now his mother would stop asking to go stay at Shyla's house. Carl was really sorry about yelling at the kids the way he had. KiKi had absolutely no control over them though, as if things weren't tense enough already. It was just as well they were leaving. At least things wouldn't look so cramped with three less people to step around. As it was, his mother's house was a mess and the garage was completely full of boxes—Pilar's boxes that she hadn't gotten around to unpacking from her move, and now Carl's.

He tried not to even think about Andrea. If he did, he got stomach cramps which led to more diarrhea. Frankly, he didn't want to ever see her again. He knew she was bad news from the very beginning when she first moved into his office. He just forgot for a moment or two. And now he was paying one hell of a price for it.

Pilar followed him around the house constantly when he was there, not letting him out of her sight. In the five days he had been staying there, he had already done enough work for three men—cleaning tile grout, washing windows, planting new shrubs and flowers. All this while working at his regular job as well.

He wanted desperately to go over to Shyla's to see her and try to talk to her, but he just wasn't sure it was the thing to do or the right time. She had made it all to clear to him in the hospital that she didn't want to see either him or his mother again. Ever. Of course, he couldn't tell his mother that. That damn attorney friend of hers with his Southern grits and milk gravy accent wasn't helping the situation any either by calling him at his mother's and asking for information. Carl had given it to him trying to make Terry Sawyer think he was a nice guy, but also because Terry had convinced him he could just as easily get the information he needed through Carl's employer if necessary. That was the last thing Carl wanted.

Surely, Shyla had had time to get over being so angry though. He could just stay for a few minutes—long enough to tell her how much he loved her and missed her. Nothing pushy. He pulled out one of his clean shirts from his mother's closet, the one that had the fewest wrinkles, and started putting it on when the front doorbell rang. It was a deputy from the Palm Beach County Sheriff's Department. He gave Carl a summons to appear in Palm Beach County Civil Court the following Wednesday morning at nine o'clock. Shyla was proceeding with the divorce.

* * *

At exactly eight o'clock Terry drove up to the large front entrance at Trégo. Miguel opened the massive wooden ornate door and stepped aside for Terry to enter. Augusto along with the servant Terry knew only as RaRa were waiting. Both were dressed formally, Augusto in a beige linen jacket and black collarless shirt with dark slacks, and RaRa in a long, flowing black dress. She wore a white gardenia in her hair, delicate and softly scented, and a strand of pure white beads. Ludicrously, Terry thought of the Grant Wood painting, *American Gothic*, only this particular image in front of him had an Hispanic touch. Terry had known that eventually he would be told what he wanted to know. But only when they were ready. Apparently, now they were ready.

"I would like for you to meet Maria Santiago Fanjul, my mother-in-law and Mariela's grandmother."

"It is an honor." Terry took the woman's offered hand. He expected her skin to feel dry and papery like so many other older people he was in contact with, but hers was warm and soft. "I believe you were once introduced to me as RaRa," he said smiling.

"Yes." Her eyes were black and piercing. "We will explain everything to you this evening." She turned and lead the way into the candle-lit dining room, the two men following her.

For the next two hours Miguel stood somewhere in the shadows, always near Maria, orchestrating the events of the meal with the other servants. They were served the traditional Cuban food of braised chicken, black beans over yellow rice, and fried plantains. Maria talked softly and melodically, stopping only when a servant entered the room to refill the glasses, remove the plates, or bring more food. Terry had already figured out most of the story. The religion, Santeria, fell out of favor with the Cuban government about the time that Maria was blessed as the high priestess of *Regla de Ocha*, an ancient precursor to the Santeria of today. If she had been a man, or *babalawo,* she would have been ostracized. As a woman, however, it meant immediate death.

The followers of *Regla de Ocha* believed that only a woman, descended from the high priestess before her, could receive the inheritance or knowledge of *Regla de Ocha.* To protect her own life and carry forward the traditions of Santeria, Maria along with several of her followers escaped to Florida, establishing a successful business in sugar cane. Even though they were no longer living in Cuba, Maria still feared for her life. If she were to die before producing a daughter to carry on the Santeria inheritance, it would have also meant the end of *Regla de Ocha,* that ancient Santerian belief that she practiced. A plan was devised: Maria would assume the role of a personal servant living at Trégo. Eventually she produced a daughter, Mariela's mother, but something was wrong. She had the darkness for which nothing could be done. The doctors told us it was a genetic disorder. Then, Mariela was born, but she too had the darkness. Like her mother who died at a young age, Mariela had only months to live. "When we knew that Mariela would soon be passing, just as her mother, Octavia, had, we petitioned the *orishas* for an answer. The *orishas* then sent Shyla to us. She was the answer," Maria said.

"Does that mean that Shyla's soul has been replaced with the soul of Mariela?" Terry asked.

"It isn't a matter of one soul being replaced or in competition with the other," Maria explained. "Now, Mariela's soul is blended with Shyla's soul, the strengths from each forming a single unit." Maria leaned back in her chair and sighed. "We are truly blessed."

Terry listened mesmerized, barely touching his food. Now he understood the meaning of the wills and why Shyla's name was on the latest one. But there was so much more being spoken than just Maria's words. He felt it the moment he entered the house. There was a sort of inaudible communication taking place on an entirely different level. When Maria finished talking, he asked, "Why are you telling me all of this now?"

"Shyla trusts you, as we do. We want her to live here at Trégo. We want her to write her book here. We want her to feel that this is now her home. You must explain it to her. In the not-too-distant future, it is she who will receive the inheritance of *Regla de Ocha*." Moving her arm in a sweeping gesture she said, "All of this will be hers." Maria glanced at Augusto who had been quiet through the entire meal.

"Shyla will need your help," he said, "as I have tried to help Maria."

"Shyla doesn't know anything about the Santeria beliefs, at least I don't think she does," said Terry.

"She knows now," said Maria. "She has the knowledge, just as Mariela did, and her mother before her. She has received the knowledge from the *orishas*. The old ways will be forever gone when I pass, but through Shyla's written words, *Regla de Ocha* will live on."

Maria's request was neither simple or casual. It would involve a total commitment on his part. There was absolutely no doubt in his mind that he would live up to that commitment.

Maria stood up then and glanced at Miguel. Terry and Augusto also stood. "We will have our coffee out by the garden," she said. A small table had already been prepared with cups and saucers. A servant was waiting ready to pour the coffee. A slight breeze stirred, scenting the air with night-blooming jasmine. Somewhere in the distance, Terry heard the mating growl of an alligator.

After Terry got home he thought over the night's events. He remembered the first time he met Augusto Fanjul. He had been an associate then, working for a large law firm for less than one year when Augusto called to make an appointment with him. After they met, it was determined that Terry would be the legal representative for the Fanjul family and business. He had been ecstatic, because it was his first big client and it had meant an immediate promotion in the firm. He was curious at the time as to why Augusto had singled him out, but he never questioned him. Now, looking back on it, he wondered if it didn't have something to do with the fact that his parents were involved to a great extent, and he to a lesser extent, in the study of soul transference and union. Maybe he, like Shyla, had been picked by the *orishas*.

It was eleven o'clock, the time he had told Shyla he would try to call her. She knew he had a dinner engagement, but he would wait until later to tell her anything about the conversation that had taken place. He wanted to be with her when he explained *Regla de Ocha* and her role in it.

* * *

Shyla's Initiative

Shyla was propped up in bed reading when the phone rang. She smiled knowing it was Terry. "How was dinner?" she asked.

"Great. Really good. I wish you could have been there to enjoy it with me."

"Perhaps another time. By the way, thanks for your note. And, yes, everything was fine when I got back."

"That's good. Which reminds me, the judge will see us at nine o'clock on Wednesday morning. Were you able to get those last two things I asked you about?"

"I have everything in a folder by the front door."

"Good. You can just bring them with you. Would you like for me to pick you up Wednesday morning and then we can ride over together?"

Shyla thought for a moment. "That means you will have to leave Naples extra early."

"I don't mind that. I get up early anyway."

After Shyla gave him the directions to her house they talked about other things. A case he had been working on for over eighteen months had finally been settled, the plantains she had bought at the grocery store to experiment with because she had never cooked them before, his lawn mower blade he had to get sharpened, and her great grandmother's clock. It was after midnight before they said good night.

Chapter Twelve

Carl awoke to the sound of a television blaring full volume. His aunt loved American television, but was hard of hearing. He looked at the clock. It was slightly past five, not even daylight yet. He went ahead and got up, knowing he would never be able to go back to sleep. He had asked for half a day of vacation time. The lawyer told him it wouldn't take long in court.

There was a knock on the door and his mother came in. She had a piece of paper in her hand and on it was written several telephone numbers with some names. "Carlos, I just don't trust the doctor I am going to now. He isn't doing anything for my pain. I want you to call these doctors and find out which ones will take my medical insurance." She put the paper on the night stand.

Carl glanced at the paper and felt his blood pressure rising. When Pilar had moved to West Palm Beach, one of the first things he had helped her find was a good health insurance company. It had taken weeks of running her around to various offices. When she finally signed up for it, she was given all the necessary and pertinent information including a directory listing the names, addresses, telephone numbers and their specialties of doctors she could go to. All she had to do was look at it. Carl snatched up the paper and tossed it on top of all the other scraps of paper he had cleaned out of his pants pockets the night before.

"So, you go to court today?"

He nodded.

"You want me to go with you?"

"No. I'm planning to go directly to the office after I leave the courthouse."

Pilar nodded and shrugged. "It will all work out." Then she added, "Don't forget to find out about the doctors."

* * *

Terry arrived at Shyla's house thirty minutes early. Not wanting to appear too eager or, worse yet, make her uncomfortable by being there while she tried to get ready, he drove around the neighborhood until it was just about half past eight. He figured that by leaving then, it would give them plenty of time to get to the courthouse and find a parking space, even during early-morning rush-hour traffic. Shyla was ready and greeted him at the door. Even though they had talked on the phone each night since she had returned to West Palm Beach, she had really missed seeing him.

"Hi, stranger," she greeted him.

"Hi, yourself," he said smiling, all the while checking to see if she seemed tense or in any way upset over what was about to take place. She wasn't. "Your home is beautiful," he said glancing around. "I got here a little early, so I drove around your neighborhood. It's nice."

"Thank you. I'll give you the nickel tour later when we have more time." She picked up the folder that had the additional information Terry had asked for and handed it to him. "I'm ready if you are."

The judge came in fifteen minutes late. Before he arrived, Shyla, Terry, and Carl were asked to wait in a lobby area where folding chairs were lined up against one wall. Carl looked like he hadn't slept in two weeks. He was wearing a suit and a tie that had a red and dark blue geometrical design. It screamed "bold." There was a button missing from his shirt. Shyla was polite, but not talkative. Terry sat between them.

When it was finally over, Shyla shook Carl's hand and wished him the best of luck. Terry knew that she meant it. Carl simply looked dazed.

"Listen, if you don't have to go back to Naples right away, would you let me take you to lunch?" Shyla asked as they were walking back to the car.

Terry didn't care when he went back to Naples. He just wanted to spend time with Shyla. "You pick out the place, and I'll pay for it."

Shyla told him which bridge to take over the intracoastal to the island of Palm Beach. They drove along the ocean until they came to Worth Avenue where she had him park in front of a small restaurant painted pink and surrounded by blooming shrubbery. It was similar to the one he had taken her to the first time he had taken her out for lunch except for the pink color. They found a table outside that was shaded by a large ficus tree and overlooking the ocean. Terry ordered them each a glass of Chardonnay.

"How do you feel now, honestly?" asked Terry.

"I feel wonderful. But somehow misdirected, like I need to be doing something really important, but I don't know exactly what."

"Did seeing Carl again upset you?"

"No, not at all."

"There was a button missing from his shirt," Terry said, examining a water droplet on his glass. Shyla had told Terry about how she and Carl had met and the circumstances. She had also mentioned how seeing his button missing from his shirt had touched a tender, sympathetic chord deep in her soul. Terry couldn't help but to think about it when he saw him earlier.

"Oh really? I didn't notice. It's the dry cleaners, you know, where he takes his shirts to get them laundered. They are brutal on buttons."

Shyla's Initiative

Terry took a deep breath. Now was as good a time as any to tell Shyla about the Fanjul's. He picked up his glass of wine and held it up to Shyla, "Here is to honesty."

Shyla listened, commenting very little, while Terry talked. When he finished telling her all of it, she started laughing.

"Shyla, are you all right?"

"I guess I am," she said between a burst of giggles. "I have been wandering around ever since the accident thinking I was a nut case. There is so much about me that is different. For instance, there is a small Cuban restaurant in town not too far from where I live. It has been there for as long as I have lived in West Palm Beach, but I had never eaten there because I didn't especially like Cuban food—until the accident. Now I go in there at least once a week. The owners are Cuban and everyone who works there speaks only Spanish. The really strange thing is that now I understand them, where before, the extent of my knowledge of the language was *si si*. But if what you are telling me is true, it explains so much." Shyla rested her arms on the table and shook her head. "Do you believe there has been a soul union, Terry?"

"Being no expert, I honestly don't know. I do believe it can happen, though. There's no reason to think it didn't happen to you."

"Now I know why they sent me the flowers." Shyla explained how she had received the red roses on the day of the private service for Mariela. "They also sent me this." She reached into her purse and pulled out the cowrie shell. She had kept it with her since receiving it.

"It is considered to be a sacred object by those who believe in the *Regla de Ocha*," said Terry. He had been spending a lot of time researching Santeria ever since that night he had dinner at Trégo. They sat looking out over the ocean.

"I'm afraid I don't know anything about *Regla de Ocha* or Santeria. I never had a reason to study it."

"Historically, it traces its roots to the African slaves, the Yorubas, who brought Santeria to Cuba. It literally means "the way of the saints," and it is based on a believer's personal relationship with African spirits called *orishas*. When Santeria arrived in Cuba, some of the ancient practices of *Regla de Ocha* were replaced by some of the characteristics of Catholicism; many of *orishas* were given the names of Catholic saints. Today believers channel their prayers by offering their gods pots full of herbs and fruits, and occasionally the blood of certain animals. The color white is considered purity of spirit, so those who practice Santeria always wear something white."

"Animal sacrifice? Is that legal?"

"The US Supreme Court handed down its ruling in the early 1990s favoring animal sacrifice for religious purposes. In the ruling it was mentioned that animal sacrifice can be traced back to the Old Testament of the Bible, that it was once part of the practice of Judaism, and that modern Islam commemorates Abraham's sacrifice of a ram instead of his son. I guess the Court felt by not allowing the followers of Santeria to have animal sacrifice would be denying their First Amendment right."

Terry passed a basket of rolls to Shyla. He knew he was giving her a lot to think about and he didn't want to make things any more difficult for her than they already were. "For what it's worth, priests in the Santeria religion are taught to humanely slaughter the animals which are used in ritual sacrifices."

"Do they ever sacrifice humans?" Shyla took a long drink of her wine.

"Never," answered Terry. "Its purpose is to offer guidance and find solutions to every-day problems. Santeria recognizes a supreme creator of the universe, but it looks to the *orishas* to watch over the world. Santerians believe that the *orishas* represent forces in nature, such as fire and water, but they also embody human spirits and have earthly traits. That's why offerings are made."

A large black grackle that had been chattering loudly on a nearby limb of the ficus tree flew closer to where Shyla and Terry were sitting. Shyla broke off a piece of bread and tossed it to the bird. "When I was a little girl, every summer I would go to visit my grandparents on their farm. There was a door leading off my grandmother's kitchen, always closed and latched, partially hidden because my grandmother used to hang her aprons and one or two sweaters on a hook next to it. There were usually several bowls or baking pans stacked in front of it as well that were too large to fit anywhere else, making the door even more unapproachable. It was the door leading to the cellar. One day I decided to open the door. The wooden stairs were steep and open; there was no banister. It was also very dark. I could just make out a light bulb attached to a cord hanging from the ceiling with a pull chain to turn it on. But it was down in the cellar at the bottom of the stairs. Finally, I sat down and scooted down the stairs, feeling my way until I reached the bottom. When I turned on the light, it caused the bulb to swing back and forth, illuminating different corners and walls, and making the cellar seem even more mysterious. There were shelves of canning jars, boxes of jar rims and sealers, stacks of empty egg cartons, gardening tools—all sorts of things. An old wooden work table had been placed in the middle of everything. Everything smelled musty and earthy, and yet, friendly. I found that I really liked the cellar."

Terry had put his hand over Shyla's while she talked. She smiled at him. "That's the way I feel about Trégo. It is a mysterious place to me now, dark and unknown. But everything within me tells me it is a place I would like."

After a while he asked, "What do you think you will do?"

"I honestly don't know. I need to think about all of this. It's just so bizarre. Doesn't it seem bizarre to you?"

Terry nodded.

"I do know one thing. I don't have the same attachment to my house that I once had. I used to spend hours in my office upstairs looking out the window at a bottle brush tree and writing. Ever since I got back from Naples, it just isn't the same."

"I can understand that. The memory of all those people stampeding through your home can't have left a very pleasant image in your mind," offered Terry.

"It isn't just that. Nothing feels right. Not my house, not my clothes, not even the food I used to eat. It's like I am sitting on that top cellar step wanting to go down, but it's the wrong cellar."

"Maybe there is a reason for it."

"Like maybe I should move to Trégo?"

Terry didn't say anything else. He personally wanted Shyla to be closer, and if she were to move to Trégo, he would be able to keep an eye out for her. He would also be able to get to know her as she was now; that is, if she wanted him to.

* * *

Carl didn't want to go to the office yet. He didn't want to go to his mother's house either. His mother would be there, a half step away from him, asking all her questions, along with his aunt watching and listening to everything. Besides, he would have to stop off at the grocery store before going to his mother's to pick up some things she needed, as if she didn't have time to go herself during the day.

Carl took off his tie and opened the top button of his shirt. The skin around his waist was starting to feel sensitive with an occasional jab of pain. He hoped that didn't mean another bout with the shingles. He had them once before when he had been married to Ana. The doctor had told him it was a virus related to chicken pox, and it was caused by stress.

After driving around for an hour or so, he finally wound up at his office, parked in his usual place in the parking lot, and went in. There were several messages on his desk, three of them from Andrea. One of them was from Ana. She was pissed because he didn't show up to fix the pool drain. He threw all of them in the trash basket. Then he checked his e-mail. There had been a staff meeting that morning; he had missed it. He scrolled down the list of other messages until he came to one he recognized as belonging to his boss. There was going to be an internal audit of the department beginning that Friday. After an informal investigation, several discrepancies had shown up involving a former employee's travel expense sheets and her purchase orders. Andrea, Carl groaned. The internal audit would be just the beginning. He had been through it before when an employee was caught stealing from the company. After the internal audit there would be outside auditors to come in, taking up room, nosing around with their questions, and using up all of his time. If the problem was serious enough, the State Attorney General could be brought in. It was next to impossible to get any work done with that kind of thing going on, not to mention the demoralizing effect it had on all the staff. Everyone would be scrutinized and under suspicion until the audit was completed.

His phone rang. It was his mother wanting to know what he had found out about the doctors. He told her he was in a meeting and hung up. He could feel his stomach starting to cramp up. He rushed down the hall to the men's room, barely making it in time.

* * *

Rosa used a tablespoon to scrape the last of the quince from the round tin and then licked the spoon as Pilar looked on. She had brought it to Pilar from Argentina, but Pilar said she couldn't eat it because of her diabetes. Pilar had gotten into a snit over it and now sat at the table opposite her sister glaring, but it wasn't Rosa's fault if Pilar had high sugar. Rosa didn't have that problem. Besides, Rosa suspected that Pilar just used the excuse of having high sugar as a convenience to play up whatever mood she was in. Too many times in the past Rosa had seen her younger sister eat desserts and other things she shouldn't, including quince. This morning Pilar was just in one of her bad moods.

It wasn't just the quince that had Pilar upset, however. Nothing seemed to be going as she had dreamed of and planned all of those years living by herself in New Jersey. She had tried calling Deena the day before where she worked, but Deena wouldn't come to the phone. Pilar only wanted to find out how she was doing and visit for a few minutes. She didn't know where Christine was or how to reach her. Carlos told her she had changed her telephone number, and he didn't have her new one. How could he not know how to reach his own daughter? She didn't understand the younger generation and their desire to have careers. Why couldn't they be content to get married and have babies? She would love to have great grandchildren. Rosa already had four.

Then there was Carlos. Why didn't he see that the divorce was the best thing for him, instead of moping around? Now they could be close just like a family should be. Mother and son, and her granddaughters once she could talk to them without so much confusion. Well, Carlos would just have to get over Shyla, and soon. The stress from it all was causing her joints to hurt, which reminded her, she hoped Carlos remembered to call those other doctors.

Pilar took the spoon from Rosa and rinsed it in the sink. The two women were planning to go to the mall after the stores opened. They would eat lunch there as well since it didn't look like Carlos would be coming home for lunch. He had told her he was in another one of those meetings and would have to call her later. She wondered if it was going to last as long as the last one did. Maybe the three of them could go out to dinner that evening when he got home. After shopping all day, she would be too tired to cook anything anyway. They could go to that Spanish restaurant her hair dresser had told her about.

When she called Carlos earlier she didn't ask him anything about the divorce. The less said about Shyla, the better, as far as she was concerned. She had never fit in and Pilar wasn't going to pretend she was sorry about the way things happened. Maybe later, after they got back from dinner, she would have a nice long talk with her son so he would understand exactly how she felt. Then maybe he could get those two daughters of his to start acting friendlier toward her.

She went to her closet and pulled out a clean dress to wear shopping. It needed to be ironed because of all the clothes Carlos had hanging on the rod with her things, crowding everything and stretching them out of shape. This didn't help her mood any. Ironing always made her perspire so. She went to the bathroom where she opened a new box of body powder. She would be glad when the hot summer months were over and the weather turned cooler, if it ever did turn cooler in South Florida.

**

Normally Jayne would have laughed at what Terry had told her, thinking it was someone's idea of a practical joke. The expression on his face, however, had said this wasn't a joke. There was a strong possibility that some sort of soul union had occurred between Shyla and Mariela at the time of the accident.

Jayne was in West Palm Beach for the day and had invited Shyla to meet her for lunch at the Ritz Carlton where she was attending a meeting. She wanted to see Shyla for herself just to make sure she was all right.

Jayne went to the dining room a few minutes early and found a table overlooking the gardens. It was quiet there, and the two of them would be able to talk privately. Moments later Shyla came in wearing a bright yellow print dress with thin shoulder straps and matching heels. Small rectangular citrine stones adorned her ears and wrist. "You look so put together," Jayne immediately told her. "I have never seen you dress in yellow before."

"Thank you," said Shyla hugging her friend. "I have never owned anything yellow before. I honestly feel like a different person." She looked at Jayne and giggled, "I guess Terry told you of my so-called condition?"

Jayne nodded. "Do you believe it?"

"I frankly don't know. There have been so many unexplained things to happen to me since that horrible night. Nothing bad, but things that I would never have thought about before the accident. Sometimes I don't even recognize myself. Take this, for instance." She indicated the *piña colada* she had asked the waiter to serve her. "I never used to drink anything but wine. Now I drink a lot of things. And coffee. Remember how I couldn't stand the taste of coffee?"

"You said it made your stomach upset."

"That's right. Now I love coffee, especially Cuban coffee. I still drink tea occasionally as well. And driving over here today. You know what the traffic is like in West Palm Beach. It's terrible. I actually balled up my fist and yelled at another driver, some old lady, for cutting me off. Do you believe what I am saying? It is almost like I have received all of Mariela's likes and dislikes, as well as some of her behavior patterns, and they have become fused with my own."

"Have you gotten back to your writing yet?"

"That is the most amazing thing of all." Shyla leaned toward her friend not wanting anyone to overhear. "All I can think about is the novel Mariela was planning to write from her short story. In the last two weeks, I bet I have written it in my mind a hundred times, the idea is so strong."

"So you will write it then."

Shyla shrugged and shook her head slightly. "I honestly don't think I have any choice in the matter."

It was late when Jayne got back to Naples. Terry had asked her to call him regardless of the time. Before getting ready for bed she dialed his number.

"Well, I can't explain it. It's like I told you before. There are so many things about her that are different—stronger, perhaps, more stated. She is still Shyla, though. Everything that I love and admire her for is still there."

"That's how I see her. Did she say anything about moving to Trégo?"

"No. Only that she wanted to write Mariela's novel." There was silence on the phone line. "Does Shyla know about Maria's will?"

"No. It would be a complete breach of ethics if I told her since I am representing the Fanjul family in the matter. Conceivably I could get into trouble for letting you see it, but I figure I have an excuse if I need it by saying I needed you as an expert to translate the thing for me and that I showed it to you in the strictest of confidence."

Jayne grunted. Something had been worrying her and she needed to tell Terry. Hopefully he would feel the same way. "I really don't think that it is anyone's business about the will or anything else that has happened to Shyla, and I, for one, don't plan to mention it ever again. Shyla is my friend, and I love her for who and what she is, no matter what."

She heard Terry let out a big sigh. "I couldn't agree with you more."

After hanging up the phone, Jayne pulled out some travel brochures she had received in the mail telling all about the vacation spots in the North Carolina mountains. It would be October before she knew it, and Shyla had mentioned how much she was looking forward to their so-called mini-vacation that first week. They were going to a place called Little Switzerland in the Blue Ridge Mountains not too far from Asheville. It was a place Shyla was especially fond of that time of year. The trees would be beautiful. Jayne had already told George about their trip so he could make his own plans.

Shyla would be fine. And now having seen her, Jayne was sure of it.

Chapter Thirteen

Shyla giggled like a teenager as she tried on the various outfits. Until the accident, most of the things she wore fell into the somewhat nondescript color families of beige, brown, gray, and dark blue, and maybe an occasional white. This was now unacceptable; none of her clothes seemed to be appropriate to wear or suitable. It felt like an entire new world had been revealed to her through the magic of color. It changed how she felt about herself as well as how she looked—and how others saw her. She was enjoying every minute of it.

The sales clerk who was helping her came into the fitting room with another arm-load of garments. "O.K. No more," said Shyla. "Otherwise I won't be able to afford groceries for the next six months." Standing in front of a full-length mirror, she held up a long-flowing dress in burnt orange with splashes of blue and yellow. It accentuated her dark blue eyes, and her entire face seemed to light up.

"I honestly believe you can wear just about any color," the clerk said. Then she pulled out a white dress from the bottom of the stack and held it in front of Shyla. It was simple in line and detail. "An understatement of elegance," said the clerk looking at Shyla's reflection in the mirror after she slipped the dress over her head, "when you need something a little special. Little white, strappy shoes on your feet. You will be all set." Shyla lifted her hair from her neck imagining what it would be like to wear such a lovely outfit to something like a dinner party perhaps or to the theater. Just a simple strand of pearls and earrings to match.

"I'll take this one too." Shyla removed the dress and handed it to the lady to put with the others she had already decided on, "but that's all."

Shyla had given up trying to figure out what was going on with her. It was easier if she didn't question it too much, but, rather, accept it, whatever *it* was. So far, there had been nothing in her life to make her fearful or cause her concern. It was all just so bewildering. And yet, she felt better from a physical sense than she had ever felt. Her attitude was positive. And her energy seemed to be endless. Whatever was happening to her, she had decided to go along with it. Deep down, she knew it was right and it was good. She also knew that she would soon be ready to start writing again. She could feel it inside of her. The characters in the novel were taking shape; the outline was formed.

Back in her car with her packages safely stored in the trunk, Shyla drove to the end of Worth Avenue and turned south on the ocean highway. She didn't want to put it off any longer; she couldn't.

According to the map, the street where the botanica was located shouldn't be too hard to find. When she did find it, she was surprised at how innocuous it looked, positioned in a small strip shopping center between a dry cleaners and a Hispanic grocery. The word *"Botanica"* was painted in black on a small white board nailed above the door.

Upon entering the shop, her immediate reaction was to the variety of scents, at once strange and yet familiar. It was then that she noticed the confusion of colorful objects and shapes around her. Shelves heavy with candles, statues and other merchandise made crisscross pathways from the front of the shop to the back. Along the way tarot cards were offered in three languages: Spanish, English and French. Special soaps promised love, money, power, and the fulfillment of other desires. Seventy-nine-cent perfumes in half-ounce bottles offered the fulfillment of other wishes. Herbs and flowers, both dried and fresh, were either stuck in water-filled containers or hanging from overhead rods. Mint, peppermint, lavender, rosemary, chamomile, rue, sage, pennyroyal, licorice, lovage, wormwood, feverfew, lemon balm—Shyla recognized them all. She pinched the dried lavender between her thumb and forefinger and smelled its calming aroma. Carved wooden figures of all sizes were everywhere. Shyla gently fondled the colorful *ilekes* that were hanging on a nearby wall, enjoying the sensation on her fingers. They were the beads sanctified by the Santerian priest or priestess and believed to protect the wearer against evil. Then, in the farthest-most corner, Shyla paused in front of a large black cauldron. She knew what was in it before she even looked. The scented aerosol sprays and burning candles almost masked the stench of the decomposing goat's head. Almost.

As though to answer her unspoken question, she heard someone say, "There is no evil in this place." Shyla turned toward the man standing behind her. "I have been waiting for your visit." The man, dressed in white, spoke to Shyla in Spanish. He must have come from the back of the shop, for Shyla hadn't seen him when she arrived. "Come this way, please." He smiled at Shyla and led her to a small room behind a drawn curtain. He motioned for Shyla to sit in the single wooden straight-back chair that was pushed to one side. The man then removed a brown leather box from a nearby table and sat on the floor, cross-legged. When he opened the lid on the box, Shyla could see several cowrie shells—sixteen in all. The man smiled at her again and then tossed the shells onto the floor. "The shells speak to me," he said quietly. "They will give me the answers you seek." Then he counted the shells that had landed face up. Again he smiled.

Several minutes later, wearing a strand of white *ileke* beads—purity of spirit, Shyla left the shop and walked back outside into the bright sunshine.

* * *

Everyone had long ago left the building. Only Carl remained behind working at his computer. It was seven o'clock, past the time he had told his mother he would be home for supper, but he just couldn't seem to make himself leave. Staying with his mother was becoming increasingly difficult, and the idea of facing another evening listening to her litany of complaints was making his bowls act up. He would rather stay at his office and work.

After a while Carl picked up the receiver of the telephone for the third time, hesitated, and then put it back down. Thinking back on it, being married to Ana hadn't been all that bad. There had been problems, but nothing they couldn't have worked out if they had really tried. They had brought two beautiful daughters into the world, for Christ's sake, and even now he and Ana continued to be friends, for the most part, if you could call it that. Ana hadn't remarried; in fact, she wasn't even seeing anyone, something he had managed to squeeze from Deena. Not wanting to give up any of the alimony he was paying her played a large part in it, he was sure. But still. Maybe she continued to feel something for him, and just maybe they could somehow start again. They might as well. When he wasn't hauling his mother around, he was over at Ana's anyway, fixing this or setting up that.

The house was nice. They had bought it and moved in just as Christine was getting ready to strike out on her own. Deena had left home a couple of years earlier when she started working as a bank teller. The house was like a reward Carl and Ana had earned for themselves after those many years of struggling and giving up things in order to get ahead. It was the home that would see them through retirement. Then, like so often happens, nothing seemed to work between them any longer. They couldn't talk. They didn't enjoy being with each other. Sex was out of the question. They just had that house. It was like payback time for all those long hours they spent apart working for the time when they could afford a beautiful home and take some time off to enjoy it. There had been sacrifices, one of them being their love and respect for each other.

Instead of being happy over what they had managed to accomplish, Ana became disappointed and bitter. Her constant nagging and unprovoked outbursts were more than Carl could take. With both daughters out of the house, there was no one else to deflect Ana's anger. Ana was a screamer, and Carl despised confrontation or being placed in an adversarial position. He found himself spending longer hours at the office and volunteering for more and more community and church activities. Anything to get him away from Ana, which, of course, resulted in more anger and more outbursts. In the end, it was Ana who actually filed for the divorce. She didn't need or want Carl any longer. Their marriage simply wasn't worth the struggle. She decided she needed to be on her own. After all, she had her own beauty shop that kept her busy. With a healthy alimony check coming in every month, she could live better than being married to Carl, and with a lot less aggravation. It was six months later when he met Shyla.

So much had happened in such a short time. He had gotten an e-mail from Andrea telling him that she and her husband were getting along better now and that she had accepted a job in Buenos Aires. The two of them would be moving the end of the month. Carl felt relieved. He wished Andrea luck wherever she went; he just didn't want her anywhere near him.

He hadn't heard from Shyla since the divorce. For a time they had been so close, and yet, that day when he saw her for the last time, with that lawyer friend of hers hovering around territorially, she was like a complete stranger. When he shook her hand, he could have been shaking anyone's hand. He didn't even recognize the feel of it. It was still soft, but it seemed a little larger somehow.

Now that Rosa had gone back to Argentina, Pilar was in full throttle with all of her demands and needs and nothing but time on her hands to think about them. She was driving him crazy. He simply had to find a way out.

Once again he picked up the receiver, this time dialing. She picked up on the third ring.

"Hello, Ana? His voice sounded too high pitched. He tried lowering it by clearing his throat. "I was wondering if you would like to go out for dinner tomorrow night. I've discovered a new Argentinean restaurant just south of here that is supposed to be excellent." She used to love eating out. He hoped she still did.

There was complete silence on the other end and then a quick burst of air like a muffled snort. "The old bitch is really getting to you, huh?"

Carl felt his stomach clench. He didn't answer. Of course Ana knew all about his break-up with Shyla and that he was living at his mother's. He was sure his daughters kept her informed. Ana had disliked his mother from the very beginning and always would, not that he blamed her. It was a shame, too, because in a lot of ways they were a like. They were both opinionated and demanding. And they both needed to be in control. There would never be any sort of reconciliation between them, though, and that was what Carl was counting on. Maybe if he and Ana could get back together, he would at least have somewhere to live, and his mother would have to find someone else to do whatever in the hell she needed. She had plenty of money; she could hire people, the way everyone else did.

"Sure, why not," Ana finally said. "Pick me up at eight."

* * *

The large, over-stuffed chair creaked and groaned under Pilar's weight as she repositioned herself in it trying to see as far down the street as possible through the living room verticals. It was the third time this week that Carlos had been late coming home for supper. She didn't mind eating late, but it was such a chore trying to keep certain dishes hot. Besides, when he told her he would be home by a certain hour, she expected him then, not thirty minutes or an hour later.

She had driven all the way over to that Cuban market on Dixie Highway just to get some lean flank steak to fix for Carlos. The least he could do was be there on time to eat it. It didn't help matters any when her sister, Rosa, called earlier in the evening from Argentina to tell her all about the little trip to some fancy resort along the coast her grandchildren were taking her on the next day. It was all Pilar could do to get Carlos to take her to the grocery store.

Carlos had been moody lately. Still recovering from his divorce, she supposed. But he needed to get over it and start paying attention to her needs. For one thing, her arthritis had been acting up more than usual, not that he noticed, and even though it had been over two weeks since she had asked Carlos to find out about some other doctors she could go to, he still hadn't done it. He probably didn't even have the list any more, after she had gone to all that trouble to write it out with the doctors' names and telephone numbers. She hadn't seen or even talked to her granddaughters either since that day they all had lunch at the Olive Garden. Carlos had taken no initiative at all in moving that situation forward. And try as she might, she couldn't reach either one of them on the phone. They were always too busy. Too busy to talk to their own grandmother.

Nothing had turned out like Pilar had expected. She thought that with, first, Ana and then Shyla out of her son's life, everything would be just as it should be. Mother and son, and two granddaughters. Well, she didn't have two granddaughters, and she barely had a son. All she had was a healthy bout of arthritis.

Her hair dresser had given her the name of a good attorney, a Cuban. He dealt in matters concerning wills and trusts. She would give him a call. For one thing, now that she was living in Florida, she needed to make out a new will anyway. He could advise her. He was probably used to hearing about parents being abandoned by their own children, not that Carlos had abandoned her. He just wasn't very attentive.

She heaved herself out of the chair and lumbered into the kitchen. She wanted to make sure the foil she used to keep the steak from drying out completely was still doing its job. After dinner she would get Carlos to take her car over and fill it up with gas. She didn't know how to do it. In New Jersey she had always taken her car to a full service station.

* * *

Jayne received the request from Maria Santiago Fanjul through Terry. Maria wanted Jayne to hold a small dinner party in her home for just the six of them: Maria and Augusto, Shyla and Terry, and Jayne and George. Maria also asked that it be scheduled for the Saturday next and that Shyla's invitation be sent to her at Trégo.

"How strange." She poured a glass of iced tea and put it on the table in front of Terry along with another one for herself. "Of course, I will be happy to have a dinner party, but it does bring up all sorts of interesting questions, doesn't it?"

Terry nodded and took a big drink from the glass. "For one thing, why send Shyla's invitation to Trégo? I know she is thinking about putting her house up for sale, but that is a long way from having it sold and her living at Trégo. For all I know, she might want to move back to North Carolina."

"And why would Maria want the dinner party here, unless it is her way of trying to help Shyla adjust to all that has happened." Jayne sat

Shyla's Initiative

down opposite Terry. "Maybe it has to do with the twin soul thing, and Maria wants to demonstrate to Shyla the Fanjul family's acceptance of both. Does that make sense to you?"

"I thought of that too. I think that's probably what it is. Maybe Maria feels Shyla would feel more comfortable with them if she is in the company of friends as well."

"Well, of course I will have the party. I think it will be fun." Jayne looked at Terry wide-eyed. "Don't you?"

"The Fanjul family doesn't exactly encourage questions. I guess we'll just have to assume the old gal knows what is happening." Terry drained his glass. "Well, I for one plan to be here Saturday after next and, hopefully, it will be with Shyla. So fix something good to eat."

After Terry left, Jayne immediately prepared the formal, hand-lettered invitations on a beautiful egg-shell linen paper. Next, she jotted down some ideas on what to serve. Jayne always believed in doing things as much in advance as possible. She could serve Cuban food which Maria and Augusto would enjoy, as well as Shyla with her newly acquired taste for the exotic and foreign. Or she could serve something that was totally American, which would please George and probably Terry. In the end she decided on a combination of both Cuban and American foods served with a wonderful California domestic wine she had recently discovered. With that decision out of the way, she went into the library and got down two of her old reference books on ancient languages. Maybe following dinner there would be an opportunity for her to converse with Maria in *Gaunche*. That should liven up the party.

* * *

Terry returned home after his visit with Jayne feeling apprehensive and unable to concentrate on work. The most frightened Terry had ever been before the age of ten was when his parents took him and his brother to the county fair at Myrtle Beach, thirteen miles south of Little River, and the Ferris wheel car he was riding in got stuck in the topmost position. It took the fair officials with the assistance of the local fire department two hours to finally bring him down to safety. Now, at the age of forty-five, his greatest fear was that Shyla would move back to North Carolina, meet someone else and fall in love, and he would never see or hear from her again. Since Shyla's divorce, they continued to talk frequently on the phone, at least once a day, and he had made several trips to West Palm Beach, presumably on matters pertaining to business, but, in fact, just to see Shyla. He didn't question her about her plans; he knew she was more than likely still sorting them through. When she was ready for him to know, she would tell him. All he could do was offer his help and support. The love was already there, it would always be there; but only if and when she wanted it.

He picked up a book thinking that reading might help to relax him when just then the phone rang. It was Shyla. "I was just thinking about you," he said smiling into the receiver.

"I've reached a decision," she said.

Chapter Fourteen

Maria once again walked through the west wing, checking for dust or anything that might look out of place. Everything was immaculate. Everything was perfect. Some of the rooms had been repainted, softening the bold, vibrant colors like purple and saffron Mariela had loved to the more pastel and subdued tones. A few new things had been purchased and brought in, such as bed linens and some every-day dishes. Shyla's taste ran toward the more sophisticated tailored look with a feminine touch. She would feel comfortable with what had been selected for her. Everything else was as it had been when Mariela lived there. Shyla would feel comfortable with that as well. Miguel had brought in the fresh vegetables and fruits earlier that day. The freezer and pantry were already stocked. On a small dark-stained table near the front door, Maria adjusted the stem of one of the red roses arranged in the crystal vase. The fragrance was sweet and welcoming. Shyla would notice. A hand-addressed invitation had also been placed on the table, next to the vase. Above the table hung a small oil painting depicting an autumn mountain scene. It would remind Shyla of the North Carolina mountains where she and her late husband had spent so many happy times. Maria smiled. Everything was ready.

Chapter Fifteen

The lane was marked by a sign, nailed to a tree, that was small and easy to miss: *Trégo: Trespassers will be prosecuted.* Shyla kept a sharp eye out, whizzing along, pushed by the traffic on the narrow road—the only road—leading across the island. Still she managed to miss the turn and, annoyed with herself, pulled over at a place called Misty Pelican Vista ("If you find yourself at Misty Pelican, you've gone too far") and headed back.

The windshield wipers squeaked unmercifully in the pounding rain, making the dreary approach of darkness even more so. She ignored the three cars already lined up behind her, unable to pass, and slowed in front of whatever appeared to be an entrance onto someone's property: a large stone marker, a bare area where the undergrowth had been whacked away, a reflector stuck in the ground. Finally, a mile or so from where she had turned around, she saw the sign, exactly as Terry had described it. By now it was close to dusk.

Shyla whipped the car off the blacktop road and through the open gates that were partially obscured by a healthy entanglement of red bougainvillea. There must have been a night-blooming jasmine growing close by as well, for its heavy scent seemed to cling to the rain-saturated air. She was arriving later than she had planned, but that was all right. She didn't have to report to anyone. No one was expecting her at any particular time. In fact, no one even knew where she was except for Terry, and he wasn't going to tell anyone. And, of course, The Guardian, if she was going to believe that story. She just didn't know yet.

For days Shyla had been bumping into walls, losing her purse in unusual places like the refrigerator, and existing in a state of general preoccupation with the way everything was developing. It had been two weeks since her divorce. Two weeks since a lot of things. Her decision to put her house up for sale, for one thing, her decision to buy a small white sports car, for another, and her decision to move to Trégo. Now that she had finally arrived, the anxiety she had felt for all those months before the accident had been replaced by an eager anticipation. Her skin tingled and her eyes felt like they were too big for their sockets, but the rib and chest pain she had associated with the exploding air bag was no longer there. It was simply gone, along with all of the uncertainty of knowing what to do.

Strangely enough, now having passed through the massive gates, she thought of the name "Eleggua." Why, she didn't know. Just like she didn't know why now unfamiliar memories filled her mind, or why now she had a craving for foods she once disliked, or why now all of her clothes seemed dowdy and too conservative and totally inappropriate, or why now she suddenly felt confident enough to leave everything she was familiar with and begin all over. Or was she? Even though she had never been to Trégo, she knew everything about it. She felt as though she were returning to the place where she had started. To where she belonged.

It was the accident, of course. Her body was healed, but her mind was still screwed up. It had to be the accident.

Shyla pressed the accelerator, encouraging her little white Miata forward, carefully avoiding low-hanging branches, broken fronds, and other vegetation encroaching on the side of the shale-covered lane. She found the sound of rain mixed with that of tires crunching oyster shells soothing, as though she were returning to the familiar sounds and scents of a place she had once loved. Through the trees she occasionally caught a glimpse, or thought she did, of a light in the distance up ahead as though beckoning to her. Or maybe it was just the reflection of her own headlights.

The lane continued to meander and twist through a thick growth of what appeared to be mangrove trees, palms, scrub oaks, and palmettos, eventually spilling out onto a large, open circular drive fronting the mansion. In sharp contrast to the encumbered path leading to it, the circular drive was completely void of any vegetation, punctuating even more the massive Mediterranean home which until that moment had been totally hidden from view. Its overwhelming size and beauty literally caught her breath, and she found herself leaning forward on the steering wheel gaping through each swipe of the windshield wiper. The outside lights had been turned on and several rooms throughout the house were illuminated as well, giving her a comfortable feeling of welcome. ("It was built in the mid-1800s and would have probably been torn down, the land subdivided and sold by now, if it hadn't been for the grandmother's insistence on keeping it in the family. It's really nothing that special though.")

Nothing that special. Slowly she eased the car forward trying to position the headlights so she could view as much of the mansion as possible. So this was Trégo. She could see the left wing of the house as well as the front facade. She counted three chimneys, perhaps four, and there was what appeared to be a stone or oolite wall just beyond the house, probably indicating a garden or courtyard. She could see a thicket of trees, cypress trees. The image of a stone altar adorned with flowers and fruits flashed through her mind. Through the noise of the rain and windshield wipers, she could hear the pounding of the ocean surf coming from somewhere beyond the house. ("Of course, it faces the ocean, and on the other side there is the inlet. So you will feel like you are on an island.")

Up on the porch of the main entrance Shyla saw an elderly woman waiting, dressed all in black except for several strands of colorful beads. RaRa, she thought. Shyla turned off the ignition and sat motionless, feeling, listening and looking at what was now going to be her new home. "Trégo." She spoke the word softly into the darkness, listening to how it sounded, absorbing how it felt. "Shyla Wishon has arrived. She has finally arrived."

About the Author

Barbara Casey, originally from Illinois, attended the University of North Carolina, N.C. State University, and N.C. Wesleyan College where she received a BA degree, *summa cum laude*, with a double major in English and history. In 1978 she left her position as Director of Public Relations and Vice President of Development at North Carolina Wesleyan College to write full time and develop her own manuscript evaluation and editorial service.

Ms. Casey is the author of over two dozen award-winning novels and book-length works of nonfiction for both adults and young adults, as well as numerous articles, poems, and short stories. Her book awards include, among many, the Independent Publishers Book Award, the Book Excellence Award, and a Pulitzer nomination. Several of her books have been optioned for major films and television series.

In 2018 Barbara received the prestigious Albert Nelson Marquis Lifetime Achievement Award and Top Professional Award for her extensive experience and notable accomplishments in the field of publishing and other areas.

Now Available!

AWARD-WINNING AUTHOR
BARBARA CASEY

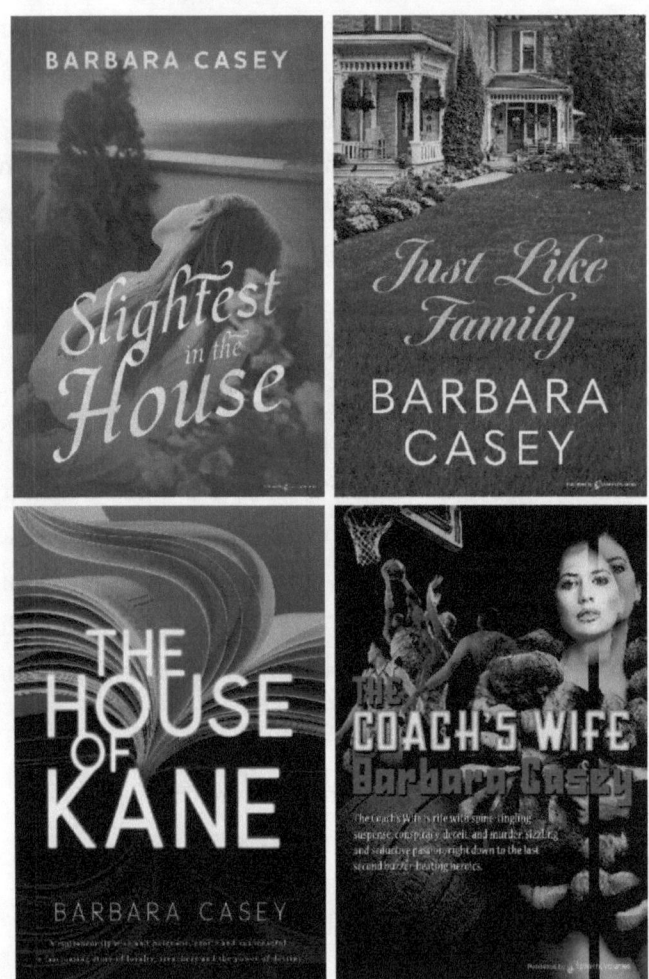

**For more information
visit:** www.SpeakingVolumes.us

Now Available!

CYNTHIA AUSTIN'S
THE PENDANT SERIES

**For more information
visit:** www.SpeakingVolumes.us

Now Available!

JACQUE ROSMAN'S
AN ACADEMIC MOM MYSTERY
Book One

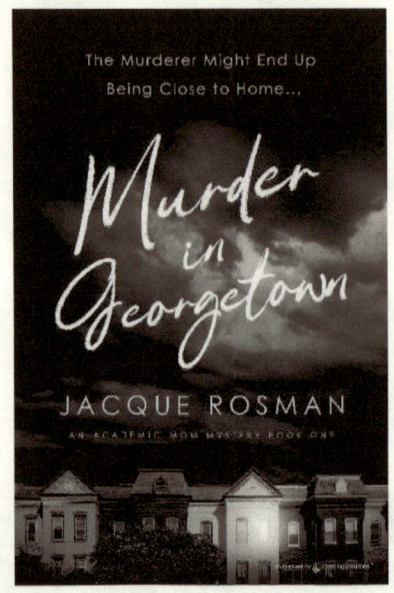

For more information visit: www.SpeakingVolumes.us